## PRAISE FOR *TWO NURSES, SMOKING*

"Midway through the title story of his dazzling new collection, *Two Nurses, Smoking*, David Means suddenly reverses course on the tale you've been reading, about two soul-weary health care workers embarking on a tentative romance."
—Jess Walter, *The New York Times Book Review*

"*Two Nurses, Smoking* is Means at his best—intelligent, often funny, always beautiful . . . This is a remarkable book not just about grief, but about the moments of brightness that punctuate it, making it both easier and, somehow, even more painful."      —Michael Schaub, *Star Tribune* (Minneapolis)

"Death, loss and the ravages of mental illness aren't the ingredients for light entertainment, but they make for a memorable reading experience in the exceptional story collection *Two Nurses, Smoking* by David Means."
Michael Magras, *Shelf Awareness* (starred review)

"[Means] explores the parameters of existence in his dazzling latest . . . Readers will revel in this robust collection."
—*Publishers Weekly* (starred review)

"There's nothing quite like a David Means story . . . Means is a genius of the fragment . . . [*Two Nurses, Smoking* is a] remarkable set of stories, which seek to destabilize the illusions of fiction even as they embrace and heighten them. How does he do it?"      —*Kirkus Reviews* (starred review)

"Infidelity, self-deception, and the volatility of memory are on display [in *Two Nurses, Smoking*]; so are commiseration, grace, and connection."     —Tony Miksanek, *Booklist*

"Means is one of the most interesting short story writers working today, shining a light on the most intimate moments."
                              —Emily Firetog, *Literary Hub*

"David Means taught many in my generation how to make the painfully idiosyncratic wonder of his short stories feel weighted like novels. In *Two Nurses, Smoking*, Means has offered us his most finely crafted, soulfully achy collection. No writer writes better about the gory gaps between folks who claim to love each other. Shockingly well written."
        —Kiese Laymon, author of *Heavy: An American Memoir*

"David Means's new stories are filled with sly wit and quiet brilliance. I left them feeling as if I'd traveled across vast territories of longing and loss led by an expert guide."
        —Jenny Offill, author of *Weather* and *Dept. of Speculation*

"The stories in *Two Nurses, Smoking* are classic David Means tales, told with brilliant and stylish precision."
                    —Emma Cline, author of *Daddy* and *The Girls*

Chris Carroll

DAVID MEANS

# TWO NURSES, SMOKING

David Means was born and raised in Michigan. He is the author of five short-story collections, including *Instructions for a Funeral*, *The Spot* (a *New York Times* notable book of the year), *Assorted Fire Events* (winner of the Los Angeles Times Book Prize for Fiction), and *The Secret Goldfish*, and of the novel *Hystopia* (long-listed for the Man Booker Prize). His stories have appeared in *The New Yorker*, *Harper's Magazine*, *The Best American Short Stories*, *The Best American Mystery Stories*, *The O. Henry Prize Stories*, and other publications. The recipient of a Guggenheim Fellowship in 2013, Means lives in Nyack, New York, and teaches at Vassar College.

## ALSO BY DAVID MEANS

# TWO NURSES, SMOKING

# TWO NURSES, SMOKING

### STORIES

## DAVID MEANS

PICADOR | FARRAR, STRAUS AND GIROUX | NEW YORK

Picador
120 Broadway, New York 10271

Copyright © 2022 by David Means
All rights reserved
Printed in the United States of America
Originally published in 2022 by Farrar, Straus and Giroux
First paperback edition, 2023

Grateful acknowledgment is made to the following publications, in which
these stories originally appeared, in slightly different form: *The New Yorker*
("Are You Experienced?," "Two Nurses, Smoking," and "The Depletion Prompts"),
*Harper's Magazine* ("The Red Dot" and "Stopping Distance"), *Granta* ("Vows"
and "Clementine, Carmelita, Dog"), *Zoetrope* ("Lightning Speaks!" and
"First Encounter"), and *The Stinging Fly* ("I Am Andrew Wyeth!").

The Library of Congress has cataloged the Farrar, Straus and Giroux
hardcover edition as follows:
Names: Means, David, 1961– author.
Title: Two nurses, smoking : stories / David Means.
Description: First edition. | New York : Farrar, Straus and Giroux, 2022.
Identifiers: LCCN 2022022684 | ISBN 9780374606077 (hardcover)
Subjects: LCGFT: Short stories.
Classification: LCC PS3563.E195 T89 2022 | DDC 813/.54—dc23/eng/20220518
LC record available at https://lccn.loc.gov/2022022684

Paperback ISBN: 978-1-250-87251-7

*Designed by Gretchen Achilles*

Our books may be purchased in bulk for promotional, educational,
or business use. Please contact your local bookseller or the Macmillan Corporate
and Premium Sales Department at 1-800-221-7945, extension 5442, or by email at
MacmillanSpecialMarkets@macmillan.com.

Picador® is a U.S. registered trademark and is used by Macmillan Publishing Group,
LLC, under license from Pan Books Limited.

For book club information, please email marketing@picadorusa.com.

picadorusa.com • instagram.com/picador
twitter.com/picadorusa • facebook.com/picadorusa

D   10   9   8   7   6   5   4   3   2

*To Genève*

# CONTENTS

# TWO NURSES, SMOKING

# CLEMENTINE, CARMELITA, DOG

A middle-aged dachshund with a short-haired, caramel-colored coat scurried along a path, nervously veering from one side to the other, stopping to lower her nose to the ground, to catch traces of human footwear, a whiff of rubber, an even fainter residue of shoe leather, smells that formed a vague pattern of hikers in the past. Some had probably walked through that part of the woods long ago. She lifted her nose and let it flare to catch the wind from the north, and in it she detected the familiar scent of river water after it had passed through trees and over rock, a delightful and—under other circumstances— soothing smell that in the past had arrived in the house when her person, Norman, opened the windows.

The wind was stirring the trees, mottling the sunlight, and she tweezed it apart to find his scent, or even her own scent, which she'd lost track of in her burst of freedom. But all she caught was a raccoon she knew and a whiff of bacon frying in some faraway kitchen, so she put her nose down and continued north again, following an even narrower path—invisible to the human eye—into thick weeds and brush, picking up burrs as she moved into the shadows of the cliffs to her left until the ground became hard and rocky.

Then she paused for a moment and lifted her head and twitched her ears to listen for a whistle, or the sound of her own name, Clementine, in Norman's distinctive pitch. All she heard was the rustle of leaves, the call of birds. How had she gotten into this predicament, her belly low to the ground, lost in a forest?

That morning Norman had jiggled the leash over her head, a delightful sound, and asked her if she wanted to go for a walk—as if she needed to be asked—and looked down as she danced and wagged and rushed to the back door to scratch and bark. At the door, she had sniffed at the crack where the outside air slipped in and, as she had many times before, caught the smell that would never leave the house, the mix of patchouli and ginger that was Claire. She was still Claire's dog. In the scent was a memory of being lifted into arms and nuzzled and kissed—the waxy lipstick—and then other memories of being on the floor, rolling around, and then the stark, earthy smell that she'd noticed one day near Claire's armpit, a scent she knew from an old friend, a lumbering gray-furred beast who was often tied up outside the coffee shop in town. It was the smell of death. Claire got that smell seeping up through her skin. It became stronger and appeared in other places until she began sleeping downstairs in the living room, in a bed that moaned loudly when it moved, and there were days on that bed, sleeping in the sun at her feet, or in her arms, and then, in the strange way of humans, she disappeared completely.

When Claire was gone, Norman began to give off his own sad odor of metal and salt, and Clementine did everything she could to make him happy, grabbing his balled socks out of the laundry pile and tossing them in the air, rolling to expose her belly when he approached, leaning against him as he read on the couch, until she began to carry her own grief.

This morning he'd dangled the leash, and, while she was waiting at the back door, he'd gone to the kitchen and got a tool from a drawer, an oil-and-saltpeter thing that made a frightening sound, Clementine knew, because once he had taken her along to shoot it upstate. (Don't get me wrong. She knew it was a gun but she didn't have a name for it—it was an object that had frightened her.) The thing was zipped into his bag when he came to the door. He stood with his hand on the handle, and she waited while he looked at the kitchen for a few seconds—minutes, in dog time—and then she was pulling at the leash, feeling the fresh air and the sun and the morning dew as she guided him along the road, deep in routine, barely bothering with the roadside odors, to the entrance of the park. On the main path that morning—with the water to the right and the woods to the left—there had been the usual familiar dogs, some passing with their noses to the ground, snobbishly, others barking a greeting. (Her own mode was to bark as if they were a threat—she was, after all, as she acknowledged in these moments, shorter than most dogs—while wagging vigorously at the same time.) There had been an old Irish setter, Franklin, who had passed her with a nod, and then a fellow dachshund named Bonnie, who had also passed without much of a greeting, and then finally Piper, an elderly retired greyhound who had stopped to say hello while his person and Norman spoke in subdued voices—she got the tone of sadness, picked up on it—and then, when the talk was over, Norman had pulled her away from Piper and they continued up the path until they came upon a small, nameless mixed-breed mutt who launched, unprovoked, into a crazy tail-chasing routine in the middle of the path, a dervish stirring up the dust in a way that made Clementine step away and pull on the leash, because it is a fact that there is just as much nonsense in the dog world as there is in the human world.

Sitting now on the rocky ground, resting, she lifted her nose to the wind and caught the smell of a bear in a cloak of limestone dust from the quarry, and inside the same cloak was the raccoon she knew, the one that had rummaged around Norman's garbage cans, and then, of course, deer—they were everywhere. Lacking anything better to do, she put her nose down and began to follow deer traces along the rocks and into the grass, a single-file line of hooves that led to a grove of pines where they had scattered, broken in all directions, and at this spot she cried softly and hunched down, feeling for the first time what might (in human terms) be called fear, but was manifested instinctively as a riffle along her spine that ran through the same fibers that raised her hackles, and then, for a second, smelling pine sap, she closed her eyes and saw the basement workshop where she sometimes stood and watched Norman, until one of his machines made a sound that hurt her ears and sent her scurrying up the stairs.

Cold was falling and her ears twitched at the memory of the sound of the saw blade. Norman was upstairs in his room staring ahead and clicking plastic keys in front of a glowing screen while she lay on old towels in the sunlight, waiting for the clicking to stop, opening her eyes when it did and searching for a sign that he might get up, get her food. Sometimes his voice rose and fell while she sat at his feet and looked up attentively, raising her paws when he stopped. Since Claire had disappeared, he left the house in the morning only to return at night, in the dark, to pour dry kibble—that senseless food—into her dish and splash water into her drinking bowl. Behind his door, the television droned, and maybe, on the way out of the house the next morning, he might reach down and ruffle her head and say, *I'm sorry, girl, I'm not such great company these days.*

As she opened her eyes, stood up, and began walking, these memories were like wind against her fur, telling her where she should be instead of where she was at that moment, moving north through the trees. The sun had disappeared behind the cliffs and dark shadows spread across the river and the wind began to gust, bringing geese and scrub grass, tundra and stone—wrapped in a shroud from beyond the Arctic Circle, an icy underscent that foretold the brutality of missing vegetation; it was a smell that got animals foraging and eating, and it made her belly tense.

Here I should stress that dog memory is not at all like human memory, and that human memory, from a dog's point of view, would seem strange, clunky, unnatural and deceptive. Dog memory isn't constructed along temporal lines, gridded out along a distorted timeline, but rather in an overlapping and, of course, deeply olfactory manner, like a fanned-out deck of cards, perhaps, except that the overlapping areas aren't hidden but are instead more intense, so that the quick flash of a squirrel in the corner of the yard, or the crisp sound of a bag of kibble being shaken, can overlap with the single recognizable bark of a schnauzer from a few blocks away on a moonlit night. In this account, as much as possible, dog has been translated into human, and like any such translation, the human version is a thin, feeble approximation of what transpired in Clementine's mind as she stood in the woods crying and hungry, old sensations overlapping with new ones, the different sounds that Norman's steps had made that morning, the odd sway of his gait, and the beautiful smell of a clump of onion grass—her favorite thing in the world!—as she'd deliriously sniffed and sneezed, storing the smell in the chambers of her nose for later examination while Norman waited with unusual patience.

That smell of onion grass was the last thing she could remember—again in that overlapping way—along with a small herd of deer, who that morning had been a few yards away in the woods, giving off a funk, and the sudden freedom around her neck when Norman unharnessed her and took the leash and she darted up into the woods, running past the place where the deer had been and, on the way, catching sight of the rabbit for the first time, chasing it while feeling herself inside a familiar dynamic that worked like this: he would let her go and she'd feel the freedom around her neck, running, and then at some point he would call her name, or, if that didn't work, whistle to bring her back; each time she'd bound and leap and tear up the hillside and then, when he called, she'd find herself between two states: the desire to keep going and the desire to return to Norman, and each time she'd keep running until he called her name again, or whistled. Then she'd retrace her own scent to find her way back to him.

It was true that since Claire had disappeared the sound of his whistle had grown slack, lower in tone, but he always whistled, and when she returned there was always a flash of joy at the reunion. Not long ago, he'd swept her into his arms and smothered her with his blessing, saying, *Good girl, good girl, what did you find up there?* Then with great ceremony he'd rolled her up into his arms, kissed her, plucked a burr from her coat, and carried her over the stones to the waterline, where he let her taste and smell an underworld she would never know: eels, seagrass, fish, and even the moon.

Yes, in the morning light she'd caught sight of a cottontail flash of white in the trees and then, giving chase, barking as she ran, followed it into the brush until she came to it in a clearing, brown with a white tail, ears straight up, frozen in place, offering a pure but confusing temptation. There they stood, the two of them. His big eyes stared into her big eyes. The rabbit darted sharply and Clementine was running with the grass thrashing her belly and then, faster, with all four paws leaving the ground with each stretched-out bound. There was nothing like those bounds! Slowed down in dog time it was a sublime joy, the haunches tightening, spreading out, and then coiling—she could feel this sensation!—as the rabbit zigzagged at sharp angles and, at some point, dashed over a creek while she followed, leaping over the water to the other side, where, just as fast as it had appeared, the rabbit vanished, finding a cove, or a warren hole in the rocks at the bottom of the palisade, leaving her with a wagging tail and a wet nose and lost for the first time in her life.

Now she was alone in the dark, making a bed in the pine needles, circling a few times and then lowering her nose onto her paws, doing her best to stay awake while the cool air fell onto her back. Out of habit, she got up and circled again in place and then lay down, keeping her eyes open, twitching her eyebrows, closing them and then opening them until she was in the room with Norman, who was at his desk working, clicking his keys. Claire was there, reaching down and digging her thumb into a sweet spot where the fur gave around her neck.

Hearing a sound, she opened her eyes. There were patches of underworld moonlight and through them deer were moving quietly. The bear was still to the north in the wind. A skunk was spreading like ink.

In the car with Norman and Claire, her own face was at the open window, the wind lifting her ears, and her nose was thrust into a fantastic blast of beach and salt marsh and milkweed chaff while, in the front seat, they talked musically to each other, singing the way they used to sing.

Something rustled in the woods. In the faint starlight, the large shadow of the bear moved through the trees. She kept still and watched until it was devoured by the dark.

She was in the bed by the window in Norman's room. He was tapping the keys. Tap tap, tap, tap.

The tapping arrived in morning light. It came from a stick against the forest floor.

The man holding the stick was tall and lean with a small blue cap on his head. *Hey, good dog, good doggie, what are you doing out here, are you lost?* The flat of his palm offered something like coconut, wheat flour, hemp, and, as an underscent, the appealing smell of spicy meat.

The man picked her up gently and carried her—*How long have you been up here, what's your name, girl?*—across the ridge of stones, through the woods to a wider path under big trees and then down, over several large stones, to the beach where he smoked and poured some water into a cup and laughed as she lapped it up, twirling her tongue into her mouth. In his hand was a piece of meat, spicy and sweet as she gulped it down, and then another, tossed lightly so that she could take it out of the air, not chewing it at all, swallowing it whole.

That was all it took. One bit of spicy meat and she reconfigured her relationship with the human. She felt this in her body, in her haunches, her tail, and the taste of the meat in the back of her throat. But, again, it wasn't so simple. Again, this is only a translation, as close as one can get in human terms to her thinking at this moment, after the feeling of the cold water on her tongue and the taste of meat. One or two bits of meat aren't enough to establish a relationship. Yes, the moment the meat hit her mouth a new dynamic was established between this unknown person and herself, but, to put it in human terms, there was simply the potential in the taste of meat for future tastes of meat. The human concept of trust had in no way entered the dynamic yet, and she remained ready to snap at this strange man's hand, to growl, or even, if necessary, to growl and snap and raise her hackles and make a run for it. Human trust was careless and quick, often based on silly—in canine terms—externals, full of the folly of human emotion.

This is as good a place as any to note that through all of her adventures, from the early morning walk on the path to the long trek through the woods and the night in the pine needles, Clementine did not once hear the loud report of a gun. Of course she wasn't anticipating the sound. Once the gun was in Norman's bag, it was gone from her mind, completely, naturally. It wasn't some kind of Chekhovian device that would have to, at some point, go off.

The man picked her up from the sand, brushed her paws clean—*It's gonna be okay. Where do you live?*—and carried her to the main trail. The sway of his arms made her eyes close. When she opened them, they were on a road and the limestone dust was strong, and there was a near-at-hand bacon smell coming from a house. He put her to the ground and let her clamber down a small cinder-block stairway and through a door and into his house.

---

In a charged emotional state, Clementine poked around the strange rooms sniffing the corners, eagerly reconnoitering—a dusty stuffed seal under a crib in a room upstairs, eatable crumbs under a bed, a cinnamon candle near a side table, a long row of records—all the while missing the freedom she had experienced in the woods, bounding through the trees, the harness gone, and beneath that, a feeling that Norman somewhere outside was still calling her name, or whistling.

All day she explored the house, pausing for naps in the afternoon sun, and retraced the activities of previous dogs, a long-ago cat, and various persons. She found pill bugs and cobwebs (she hated cobwebs) in the corners, and on a chair in the dining room, small plastic bags of something similar to skunk grass and spider flowers—not exactly onion grass, but still worth close attention.

That day, Clementine came to understand that the man's name was Steve. Later in the afternoon, a woman named Luisa arrived and spoke a different language—no words like *sit*, or *walk*, or *good dog*, or *hungry*—to which she paid close attention, partly because Luisa had a smell similar to Claire's, gingery and floral with a faint verdant, bready odor that—Clementine felt this, in her dog way—united them in a special way. There was also the way Luisa rubbed her neck, gently and then more firmly, using her thumb as she leaned down and said, *What should we call you?* And then went through many beautiful words until she settled on *Carmelita. Carmelita*, she said. *Carmelita*.

Even in her excitement over her new home, Carmelita was experiencing a form of grief particular to her species. There are 57 varieties of dog grief, just as there are—from a dog's point of view—110 distinct varieties of human grief, ranging from a vague gloom of Sunday afternoon sadness, for example, to the intense, peppery, lost-father grief, to the grief she was smelling in this new house, which was a lost child (or lost pup) type of grief, patches of which could be found in the kitchen, around the cabinets, near the sink, and all over the person named Luisa. It was on the toys upstairs, too, and as she sniffed around she gathered pieces together and incorporated them into her own mood.

Resting in the moonlight that night, on an old blanket in the room with the stereo speakers, she kept her eyes open. An owl hooted outside. A faraway dog barked. A distant rumbling sound, along with a screeching sound, began in the distance and gradually grew into a high-pitched screeching and clattering, a booming roar that was worse than thunder, and then it tapered off, pulled itself away into the distance, and disappeared.

The light came on and Steve rubbed her belly—*It's just a train, sweetie, you'll have to get used to those*—and then, in the dark again, she detected a mouse in the corner, erect on two feet, holding and nibbling on something. When she growled it disappeared into the wall. The light came again and Luisa rubbed her head and belly. Then it was dark again and to soothe herself she brought out from one of the chambers in her nose the smell of onion grass.

———

Days passed. Weeks passed. Carmelita settled into her new life. Some days, Luisa was in the house, moving around, sitting at the table with the smell of green stuff, dangling a bag of it in front of Carmelita's nose so she could sniff and open her mouth and gently clasp—she had learned not to bite the bags.

One afternoon, Steve took her into the woods, along a small trail, and through a fence to an open spot. She lay and watched as he dug with a shovel, cut down stalks, and stopped to smoke. (She liked to snap at the rings he made, to thrust her nose into the smell that tangled up and brought the sudden overlap of memory: Claire in her bed smoking, and the strange smell of the cans under the workbench in Norman's workshop.)

In the evenings, they ate at the table by candlelight and talked about someone named Carmen. Each time the word appeared, the smell of grief would fill the room. The scent was all over the house, in different variations. She even found it on the thing that Steve carried when he left the house in the morning, a leather satchel with a bouquet of iron and steel, clinking when he hefted it up—*So long, Carmelita, see you after work, gotta go build something*—an object always worth examining when he came back to the house because it carried an interesting array of distant places, and other humans.

Sometimes they took her for a walk to the woods, or down the road past the stone quarry to a park where children played and other dogs hung out. She became friendly with the dogs there and they exchanged scents and greetings. Her favorite, Alvy, a bulldog with a playful disposition and a scratching issue, came to the house one evening and they slept together in her bed, side by side. He snorted and sneezed and coughed in his sleep. When he sneezed—his massive nose was beautiful—he emitted a cornucopia of aromas, mint weed, leathery jerky, Arctic vegetation, even a hint of caribou—essences he had drawn in from the northern wind and stored for future examination.

Winter came. Snow fell. The ice smell from the north became the smell outside. When Carmelita went out in the evening—her belly brushing the snow—she kept to the path and did her business quickly, stopping only for a moment to taste the air. Then she dashed back to Steve in the doorway, the warmth of the house pouring around him into the cold blue.

One night there were cries from the bedroom upstairs. She got up—noting the mouse—and went and saw them naked together, wrapped in the familiar bloom of salt and, somehow, a fragrance like the river underworld. When they were finished they brought her up onto the bed. There was a hint of spring in the air that night, and the next morning; the wind shifted and the ice smell from the north was replaced by southern smells—one day faint forsythia and crocus, another day Spanish moss and dogwood, magnolia, morning glories, and another the addition of redbuds, and, of course, cypress, all these smells drifting in a mirepoix (no other human word will do) of red clay and turned rich farm soil that told the animal world that green was coming.

When the weather was good she would go out to the back deck—passing through the little door Steve had installed—and rest her chin on the wooden rail, looking out over the water, watching the birds in the sky, as she turned the wind around in her nose.

One morning there was another presence in the house, a small thump in Luisa's belly, a movement. Carmelita put her head down and listened, hearing a white liquid fury, along with the thump, while her tongue—licking and licking Luisa's skin—tasted the tangy salt of new life.

That night she woke in darkness—the moon gone, no moon at all—to the sound of a raccoon crying. Through the window over her bed the strong southern wind slip-streamed, and when she fell back asleep she was free, chasing the rabbit (if you had been in the room, you'd have seen her paws twitching as she lay on her side), bounding through soft grass, inside the pursuit. The rabbit froze, ears straight and still, and offered its big, pooling eyes. They stood in the clearing for a moment, Carmelita on one side, the rabbit on the other. The air was clear and bright and the sun was warm overhead. Then the rabbit spoke in the language of dog. The rabbit spoke of the sadness Carmelita sometimes felt, a long-stretched-out sense of displacement that would arrive, suddenly, amid the hubbub of the house, the leather satchel fragrance, the thump in Luisa's skin—that heartbeat—and the memory of Claire. It spoke loudly of all the things that had gone into the past and all of the things that might, like a slice of meat, appear in the future, and then it dashed off to one side, heading toward a mountain, and with a bark

(Carmelita did bark, giving a dreamy snap of her jaw) she was back in the chase, moving in gravity-free bounds over velvety grass until, with a start, she woke to darkness, staring around the room—a faint residual pre-dawn marking the windows and, once again, the mouse on its hind legs, holding something as it gently nibbled.

The end of spring came and the air filled with a superabundance of local trees, grasses, flowers, and pollen. Some days, the air was neither north nor south. A newborn was in the house, too, gurgling and twisting, crying at night.

One afternoon, the house quiet, Carmelita went onto the deck to air and sun. At the railing, her chin on the wood, she examined the wind coming from the south and as she sniffed she caught and held Norman's smell. It was faint. In human terms it was not a smell at all—a microscopic tumbleweed of his molecules. But it was there. She caught it and held it in her nose, in one of the chambers, and turned it over like a gemstone.

That night the rabbit did not pause at the end of the glade and instead the chase went on and on, weaving around until she woke up in the darkness, and to soothe herself, she sat up and examined the little bit of Norman's smell she had stored in her nose. (Again, this is just a translation. There wasn't, in any of this, a concept of causality, and the smell of Norman in the air alone, mixed into a billion other smells, wasn't enough to make her dream of escaping to the woods to trace her way back to her previous origin point. She was perfectly content in her life with Steve and Luisa and the baby, walks in the woods, good food, lots of fresh meat, even on occasion the spicy meat. That tiny bundle of molecules that smelled like Norman was just something to ponder, to bring back out.) Dawn was breaking and she got up and went to the bedroom, clicking her long nails, to listen to Steve and the baby.

One night in August she was chasing the rabbit again, a ball of white movement that pulled her along a stretch of the main path that she had traveled many times. As she ran she passed familiar pee-spots: picnic-bench legs, trash cans, bushes. The rabbit didn't zig, or zag, but was running in a straight line, undaunted, and because of this she felt a new kind of fury, an eagerness that drove her across the wide parking lot, past cars and people, with the wide river glassy and quivering to the left of her vision—everything in a dreamlike way pulled into the vortex of her singular desire, nothing at all playful this time, so that she kept her head down and plunged ahead. Then she was up the hill—completely familiar—and along a stone path to the door of the house where the rabbit had stopped and turned, twitching, standing still, as if offering itself to her. In a single fluid motion she clutched it in her rear paw, twisting hard and then, when she had her chance, she got to the rabbit's neck, clamped down, and shook it until it stopped moving and then shook it some more, taking great pleasure in its resistance to the motion of her neck, and then, as she was tasting the bloody meat, gamey and warm, there was the sound of Steve speaking, and she was on her blanket, which she had pawed all the way across the room. It was morning. He was in the doorway to the kitchen with a mug of coffee in his hand. *You must've been dreaming*, he said. *Your little paws were moving.*

Did one dream foretell another? Was it possible that the dream indicated what was to come? Of course she would never think of it that way because she wasn't bound by the logic of causality; the dream of the rabbit was as real as her waking state, so it overlapped with what happened one afternoon, a Saturday late in the summer, when Steve took her for a long hike along the path. (He never took her too far down the path because he didn't want to give her up. He had made a half-hearted attempt to locate her owner, asking around, looking at posts on the internet, until he was persuaded that no one in the area had reported a missing dachshund. But then one day at the Stop & Shop on Mountain Road, on the community bulletin board, he saw her photo. But by the summer, the dog was part of the family, and it seemed important—in some mystical way— that she had appeared in the woods before Luisa became pregnant.)

Once again it is important to stress that Carmelita's world is composed of fibers of sensation caught like lint in a web of her neurons, a vivid collection of tastes, luminous visions, dreams, and even, in her own ways, hopes and grief. Enter her nose, the enfolded sensors a million times more sensitive to odor than your own; imagine what it was like for her to hold, even as a clump of molecules, the distinctive smell of

Norman, along with every thing she had ever encountered arrayed like a nebula swirl, spinning in a timeless location.

On the path, she pulled on the leash, feeling big. It was a perfect day, with a breeze that carried not only the usual scents of the sea but of the city, too: streets and car exhaust and pretzel stands and oniony salsa and baking bread.

At a turn in the path the wind funneled along the rock and narrowed, bringing together several streams. In this wind she detected Norman's smell again, just a trace. Steve often let her loose for a few minutes at this spot where the trail was quiet and the trees were sparse. Like Norman, he called and whistled her back, but he didn't wait as long, most of the time, and the dynamic was somehow different.

As she ran up through the woods, not really chasing anything—although of course the rabbit dream was still fresh—she was surprised in a wide clearing by a rabbit in the grass ahead, eating clover, unaware of her presence. She drew closer, barked, and the rabbit froze and then dashed away, making a zigzag, leaping across a creek.

With joy and fury she ran, entering freedom. It was a smart old rabbit, larger than the one in the dream. It disappeared ahead while Carmelita kept running, skirting the creek, slowing down to nose the ground.

It was here that she caught Norman's smell in the air again, stronger than before, a distinctive slice of odor coming through the woods, not just Norman but his house and yard, too. It came strongly, in a clear-cut, redolent shape, so she ran toward it, tracking and triangulating as it appeared and then disappeared. A flash of brown dog through the grass and then the woods, her instincts making innumerable adjustments as she went over the rocky ground, through another grove of trees, pulling away from Steve, having passed beyond the familiar dynamic as the pull of the voice behind her was counteracted by the scent ahead.

It was a matter of chance that Steve had been on the phone with Luisa, talking about the baby, about diapers or formula. On this day the wind was just right and Clementine was fifty or so yards behind a certain boundary line, not ignoring the sound of Steve's voice, distant but clear, calling her name, but overwhelmed by the scent ahead. Simply put, the smell of Norman prevailed over the sound of Steve.

I wish I could make words be dog, get into her coat and paws and belly and ears as she ran, slowing down on the main trail, passing the picnic tables, the trash bins, catching now and then the familiar fragrance of home, but also, by this point, her own trace of scent on the asphalt where she had passed a hundred times long ago. If I could make words be dog then perhaps I could find the way to inhabit the true dynamic, to imagine a world not defined by notions of power, or morality, or memory, or sentiment, but instead by pure instinct locked in her body, her little legs, as she trotted up the hill and along the wall and, when the wall disappeared, cut across manicured grass, past the sign to the park, another great spot to pee, then up the road—staying to the side as she had been taught—to the driveway, stopping there for a moment to sniff.

Out on the back porch Norman was at a table under a wide green umbrella, working. Music was coming through the open door. His neck was stiff and he had his hand up and was trying to work out a kink. He sighed and was standing up to stretch when he heard her bark, once, a big bark for such a small dog. Then he had his arms out and was running and she was running, too, with her body squirming around her flapping tail until he was near and then, with another yip, yip, yip, she was on her back with her belly up, bending this way and that, waiting for his hands, because that was all there was at that moment, his hands lifting her up, lifting, until, still squirming and crying, she was pushing her face into his face, licking and licking as he spoke to her, saying, *Oh girl I missed you so much, I missed you, I let you go and started missing you the second you were gone, and when you were gone I knew I had to go on*, and then there was a burst of something beyond the wind itself, beyond the taste of meat, and the two of them were inside reunion; even in that moment she was aware that his smell had changed, and she was still dancing on her paws as she went into the house to investigate, checking the floorboard beneath the sink, going from room to room, from one corner to the next.

One day in the fall, keeping the leash tight, he took her back along the path to the spot where she had left him. It might've been that day, or another, when she caught Steve's scent in the wind, the baby's, too, and then, another time, Luisa's distinctive scent. In her dreams the rabbit still appeared from time to time, and she ran and leaped and bounded between earth and sky, hovering in bliss and stillness that seemed beyond the animal kingdom. Often, at the end of a long-dreamed chase she met the rabbit and they watched each other from their respective sides of the clearing, frozen inside the moment, speaking with their eyes of the tang of onion grass and the taste of spicy meat.

# ARE YOU EXPERIENCED?

They dropped late in the morning and then sat for an hour silently waiting for the kick in Billy's boardinghouse room, the grove of aspen trees on the edge of the field outside quivering in the summer breeze. The house was situated along the old road to the beach, not much more than ten miles from Lake Michigan. Inside, she sat looking at the poster Billy had tacked to the wall: a cartoon figure with a big leg extended, presenting an oversized shoe, and, below the heel, the words *Keep On Truckin'*. She was waiting for it to move, which it did, eventually, dancing in a way that seemed remorseful, trying to lure her in, until it turned into an aberration that somehow mirrored Billy himself, thinning out into a slim boy, with a never-ending array of plans, brilliant with his own energies, performing a little gyrating dance—the heavy shoes falling away, becoming dainty little feet (because Billy did have small feet), the hand waving at her to come on in, to join the fun, the way you'd expect an older man to lure a girl in—and she was a kid that summer, just sixteen, and Billy was at least nineteen and, unbeknownst to either of them at the time, about to head off to war.

Billy held himself over her dramatically, tossing back his hair, gazing with his blue eyes, giving out a single hootlike laugh when he came. When he was in bed, and high, he was a gentle and beautiful boy, with a faraway look in his eyes, and irresistible sandy blond hair, long and tangled. (Some said he looked a little bit like Jim Morrison, but, really, the resemblance lay in the way he moved, suddenly swaying his hips in his leather pants, radiating a charisma that seemed on the very edge of violence, launching into fits of jubilation.) Part of what held her in his thrall, she'd later think, was the way he seemed able to grapple time into submission by proposing schemes; he operated on constant speculation, always heading into the future, and that night after they made love, as they came down from their highs, he flipped onto his side and began talking about reality, about prospects for cash, about keeping their experiment—as he called it—in alternative consciousness up and running and financially viable.

She listened as plans emerged from Billy in soliloquies that sometimes lasted for hours: he rambled on about a sad gas station—the kind with old pumps and a grease pit—he might rob outside Alpena. A package store near Benton Harbor, set back among weeping willows, that was dying for a stickup. A blueberry farm near the Indiana border that would offer easy pickings if they were ever blighted with hunger. He spoke of these plans using the words he had acquired during his year at a prep school out east before he'd returned home to work for a year at Checker Cab. As he liked to explain it, he had come home and begged his parents to disown him, saying, Please, please, let me go, cast me out, I beg of you, go down to the police station and list me as incorrigible, if you do anything. I've always wanted to be incorrigible. Do it for the sake of our lineage, for the entire family right down the line. Cast me out in honor of the toil and tribulation of our forefathers. In honor of the original Miles Thomas, who never foresaw a guy like me, a long-haired hippie. Not in his wildest fantasies.

Beside her that night, in bed, he began to talk out his latest scheme: My uncle Rex and aunt Minerva were farmers, he said. But now they live in the city of Lansing. We'll distract my uncle, get him talking, and I'll go up and get the box of cash he has up there under the floorboards, the old farm money he just doesn't have the heart to spend. Money that came from the soil, and all that, because he lost his farm a few years back and he's still not over it, so it's just sitting there, with no real use.

She listened and sank deeper into the bed, wondering how they'd pull up and away from the coziness of the room, with the darkness outside and dawn scratching at the horizon. Eventually, they found the energy, got up and pulled on their jeans, got dressed, and scrawled a note for the landlord: *Dear Dan: Went on an adventure to re-establish our funds. We will be returning by evening, and upon our return we will be fully equipped to reimburse you for the back rent. Faithfully yours, Meg and Billy.*

When they got to Lansing the sun still wasn't up, and the heavy government buildings were straining to materialize out of the dark, their white limestone walls emitting an eerie iridescence while a few sad orphaned houses stood nearby, shabby and out of place, shedding shingles and curlicues of lead paint. Billy's uncle lived in one of these, just down from the Board of Water & Light building, on a plot of land held above the sidewalk by a crumbling retaining wall.

I'm really not sure about this, she told Billy as they swung up the driveway and spotted a brutal-looking farm implement, hook-shaped blades attached to a long wooden handle, leaning against the side of the house. She stared at it and glanced around for signs of movement. Billy looked the house over, took a drag on his cigarette, and began to explain: We're not going to steal, if that's what you're thinking. You've got to understand that. We're not the types to go in and take something from old folks, not at all. We're upstanding end-of-the-era hippies who just need some help, that's all, so look at it like that, Meg, look at it like a simple thing, like seesawing, or jumping jacks, or doing cartwheels. We're not going to upset the status quo, because money passed between family members sustains stability.

Billy would've gone on that way if she'd let him, waxing philosophical, bending the truth, trying to fit the round peg of their need into the square hole of his uncle's life, so finally she said, Let's go on in and say hello, and she got out of the car, closed the door softly, and went up to the porch.

At the front door, he had his knife out and was sliding it around the latch, flicking it urgently, until there was a click and the latch gave, opening into a stale darkness, a vestibule filled with the smell of wet wool, rubbing ointments, dust, moth flakes, and furnace oil. A door led to a large hall with a stairway that went up past a stained-glass window. They stood for a moment at the foot of the stairs, listening to the silence of sleeping inhabitants, until Billy called up, saying, Uncle Rex? Aunt Minerva, Uncle Rex, Aunt Minerva? From upstairs there came a grunt, the clearing of phlegm, a cough or two, more grunting, and then a voice that said, Who's that? Who's there? It was a tart central-Michigan farmhand voice, confined within the nose. (Meg didn't know it at the time, but she was hearing the intonations of a widower, the voice you'd hear from someone interrogating himself in the mirror with total contempt: a voice that made complete sense when the old man finally came down the stairs, dressed in a tattered old maroon robe, and presented a toothless mouth set in a gaunt face.) Staying on the bottom step, he looked at Billy, coughed twice, and said, What the hell do you want from me?

Billy tossed the hair out of his eyes and said, We were just in the neighborhood and thought we'd pay a friendly visit to say hello and see how you were and how the crops are this year.

A look of thoughtfulness entered the old man's face, and while his lips mulled his answer he went to the window, parted the curtains, and gazed up at the sky visible between the buildings.

Since when did you ever give a damn about farming?

I've got farm blood and a farming soul, Uncle Rex, Billy said. So get the coffee going and then come back to the parlor and fill me in on the details, give me a complete crop report, the whole thing, right down to the latest commodity update, or whatever. I'm eager to hear. Meg wants to

hear, too. There's nothing like farming. It's the only respect-
able profession left, that's for sure, and there are plenty who
are returning to the soil, Uncle Rex. You know me well
enough to know I've got farm blood. I'll buy that farm
back, rebuild it, and get it up and running again. You won't
have to do a thing but sit in your chair on the front porch
and give me occasional advice.

Uncle Rex went down the hall to the kitchen and began banging around making coffee while they stood in the
parlor amid the clutter of knickknacks and tchotchkes, old
souvenirs from across the country; spoons and miniature
statues; a plate that said "Kentucky, Abraham Lincoln Birth-
place" above an etching of a log cabin; another plate that
said "Virginia" below a gold-leaf miniature of Monticello;
a horseshoe from Wisconsin with the words "Good Luck."
At the windows, heavy drapes held back the dawn light. A
velour love seat, two small straight-backed chairs, and, in the
corner, against the wall, a pump organ.

Billy looked at the pump organ, said, Oh, yeah, I forgot
about that. Then he sat down and began pedaling, filling
the bladder with air until the instrument was wheezing and
panting. He continued pumping, throwing his head back
dramatically, holding his hands up above the keys until finally he unleashed an organ riff, *da da da, da da da dadada*,
and began singing the Doors song "Touch Me," twisting
himself down on the little stool, wagging his head around,
consumed with the music.

The percolator is going, the old man said, materializing
suddenly in the doorway. The coffee should be ready shortly.

Billy got up and went to him, told him to sit, and then

said, What about the farm? Give me the lowdown, please. I need to know everything so I can go and help. I'll hire out the combining to Hank. I'll get the whole thing operating, and then I'll come and get you and Aunt Minnie and bring you over, he said.

Your aunt's dead, the old man said.

What? Aunt Minerva's dead?

She died peacefully in her sleep. Last year. I woke up and she was gone.

When, exactly, was this?

I believe it was last July.

Jesus, no one told me a thing, Billy said. I'm sorry. Really, Uncle Rex. I'm out of the loop. I didn't know or I would've come and said a few words at the service or something.

There wasn't any service, he said. Her ashes are upstairs in the bedroom.

Well, in that case, you just go ahead and give me the skinny on the farm, Billy said. Just lay it all out, Uncle Rex.

The old man cleared his throat and began to speak, going into detail about his farm and its operation and the price of feed corn on the Chicago exchange, and the crooked Detroit bank, and the seven-year drought, starting back in '51, that caused a plague that spread over the land. As he spoke, a wistful tone entered his voice. You'll want to rebuild the barn, make it a post-and-beam mortise-and-tenon with queen posts, and don't put a ridgepole in to support the rafters, you won't need that, and put plenty of ventilation louvres along the forebay walls, and get one of those steel Martin silos in, too, and maybe a manure-cleaning system, and clear out the burdock growing through the windows, and the stalls will need new railings, and the corn crib needs new chicken wire, and the old wind pump needs lubrication and a new valve, and the tractor needs a new camshaft; you'll want to intercrop carrots with the rye and barley, get them in close to protect the young seedlings; and so on and so forth, while out in the kitchen the percolator sputtered.

When Meg got back from the kitchen with the coffee, the old man was sitting alone in the parlor expounding on soil types and the history of soil itself, the glacial loess deposits and how Paw Paw soil was better than the upstate junk spodosol, with a pure O horizon, the best you could hope for. Then he talked about soybean rust and luck farming, as opposed to chance farming, as his father had called it. If someone had been there taking notes, they might've reconstructed the farm in its entirety, from the foundation of the farmhouse itself to the rafters of the barn and to the fields, which the old man insisted were square and stately, just outside of Paw Paw, in parcel no. 55, state of Michigan, Van Buren County, a farm that sent its produce to the granary in Dowagiac, which in turn was freighted to the exchange in Chicago, just one more load from the hinterlands thrust into the great maw of commerce. From the way he was talking, it seemed he was determined to unfold the entire history of agriculture from the first primal seed on, because he was still speaking as they left the house, mumbling something about cut nails, circa 1850, and then a few words about the use of clapboard peaks as a way to ward off shingle damage. His voice was bright, happy to be drawing upon past experience, making something from words, at least, detailing the material of his former life while they went out to the car, got in, started the engine, and drove up the wide Lansing streets.

He was still talking while in the car they pried open the cash box and saw the tightly bound stacks of green, neatly arranged, with tags on them that named the years they were earned. Hard-won money that he'd hoarded and hidden away from his creditors at the bank.

That's wholesome cash, Billy said. It's money that won't mind being spent. It's not from a downer source. It's not factory money, or slave money. That green came out of the soil itself, the bountiful fucking fruit of Mother Earth. That's money that came out of sun and sky. There's no guilt in this money because it's devoid of weight, he said, as she counted it carefully, leaving the tags on each stack in case they wondered what year they were spending. No, that's money that came from sunlight and air and dirt, nothing else.

Back in Billy's room that night, they were speculating about Uncle Rex. Was he still there, ten hours later, in that house in Lansing, continuing to lay out the statistics and data of his farm? Outside, the wind was lifting through the fields, turning up the silvery leaves on the aspens. In the clouds to the west, heat lightning fluttered and laced. All day the heat had thickened. It would break soon. In a few minutes, most certainly, they'd be in the middle of a storm. Everything would cool down and shift.

I think he's sitting in that parlor in that chair, rattling on. I'm sure of it, Billy said. We got him started, but it was just the beginning. Uncle Rex is a storehouse of wisdom

and knowledge on the subject of his farm, he said, leaning down, plucking seeds, rolling joints atop the Hendrix
album cover. His idea was to roll twenty fat joints and hand
them around in the morning as a goodwill gesture, to open
up the hearts of his customers. He sprinkled and rolled,
sprinkled and rolled, stopping only to lick the papers and
to smooth and tighten, working with a fantastic efficiency,
cuffing the loose weed with the side of his palm, keeping it
neatly in the center of the album cover, obscuring the circle
with Hendrix and his band. Yeah, for sure. Uncle Rex is
still talking up a storm, but he's closing in on the end now.
He's getting to the finest of particulars. He'll be too tired
to talk much longer. He's building up to the grand finale.
He's talking about the financing. About the interest rates,
farm subsidies, and the Nixon administration. He's talking
corn prices in the month of May, the Year of Our Lord
Nineteen Sixty-one. That's when it all came down for him.
He's talking up the numbers, big-time, and the fact that he
had to take out a second mortgage on the farm. Most likely,
right about now, he's getting to the part about walking his
property line from point to point, and how he likes to stand
there on the western side, at the windbreak of oaks, and
connive over how he might force the Nugent farm into a
buyout. The old fuck was always trying to buy the Nugent
farm. He hated Nugent.

Billy went on like that, expounding on Uncle Rex's
story, until suddenly, through the rattle of his words, it became clear to her (and it did come on like that—a fearsome
revelation, a sudden sharp insight that she would carry with
her into the future) that he and his uncle had the same

habits of mind, the same inclination to fall into a ramble, a widower's intonations. It wasn't just the drugs, either. Cosmic forces wouldn't save him from the kind of fate his uncle had faced, and she felt sure he'd be there one day, husky-voiced after telling his tale in the same way, going on and on about it for days on end after some fuckups came in to loot *his* cash box. Instead of farming, he'd be talking about drugs: the price of a lid in Bay City back in the day; dime bags and shortages in the Upper Peninsula; the problems of getting the Detroit supply line going during the aftermath of the riots; how hard it was, back in the mid-seventies, to get a dependable connection in Chicago. He'd be going on in that soft, speculative voice, landing hard on the specifics, the price of STP in the Keweenaw Peninsula; the Traverse City acid freak-out; the Grand Rapids meth crisis; the Gaylord sheriff's department's pot bonfire; and he'd mention her, too, little Meg Allen, who got slapped in the face by her mother and took off on an adventure, and he'd say that he had this old lady back then who was useful, businesswise, this girl, just sixteen and in thrall to his body and voice; a girl who made wild love and was pure as soap. Then he'd go deeper into his story, with the most spectacular precision, about the way his tongue tasted when he was tripping and the various vagabond colors that came flowering up out of the quaking aspens as they lifted their wet leaves in the lightning.

On the bed that night, as Billy rolled his joints and kept on speaking, ignoring the wind that was swishing the curtains, bringing the smell of the trees and the lake inside, all this became clear. While the stacks of cash on the bed beside her ruffled and the tags—each with a date, 1955, 1959, 1960—fluttered. While his fingers busily swept the pot into little formations. While the breeze tried to brush the pot off Jimi Hendrix's face and onto the bedspread, she imagined him alone in some dusky house, baking in an eternal heat, in Kansas or Nebraska, hiding out from the law, which had long since stopped looking for him, in an age that was cleaner and tidier, working himself into a fit over what had happened on this day, August 5, 1971. He was alone in that house, without her and without love, trying to reconstruct what was gone while those who had started him speaking in the first place, who had offered up the initial opening question, were long gone with his loot, the earnings of an entire life, heading west toward the California coast, leaving a cloud of dust in their wake, laughing at the image of him back there, somewhere, still rambling on about his life.

# TWO NURSES, SMOKING

## FROM A WIDE VANTAGE

Two hospital workers, somewhat lonely-looking figures, taking a smoke break, back behind a trailer, leaning toward each other as they talked softly beside a row of neatly trimmed bushes. One had long hair and thin, pale arms that dangled from her scrubs. The other was big, burly, with a tattoo on his arm. Even that day in June—if you paid close attention, driving past—you might've seen desire in the way she pointed her toe and dug it into the dusty concrete while she listened to him, or you might've noticed the way he swayed as he talked, because he liked to riff on the subject at hand, and, lately, the last few times, when she visited with the trailer, he had expounded upon the recent news: a serial-killer nurse who had confessed to murdering, somewhere in Pennsylvania, at least a dozen patients. She, for her part, added a little commentary here and there, because it was a shared story that somehow seemed to make the job a bit easier, the kind of bullshit story that you'd tell to kill time, and she liked his deep, no-nonsense tone, which, she thought, might've come from his stint in the army. He had green eyes that became deeply serious when he was listening.

## THE BOND

Began to form in the way they both moved during the breaks—in the solitude they sought between the bushes and the long flank of the trailer, a dirty sliver of parking-lot curb where cigarette butts and litter had blown up. Between them was a secretive energy, a conspiracy formed out of a mutual history. (Or maybe the conspiracy formed a sense of mutual history. Maybe it wasn't so simple.) As a kid she had lived in one of those motels, Holiday Court, that had turned itself over to long-term renters—folks who paid by the week but did so year in and year out when they could, building an easy camaraderie, fighting in the parking lot, spilling blood, bringing the police—the daughter of a fuckup mom with zero parenting skills. A kind, encouraging counselor at her high school named Mrs. Hargrove, who gave her hope, urged her to take a heroic leap to community college, and then nursing school on a scholarship. He'd grown up in Nevada near a town called Ely, on the Shoshone reservation, without a father, spending a lot of his time alone in the countryside, staying out of his mom's way, and then, suddenly, they'd moved east to a trashy apartment in Newburgh, New York, with a new dad who liked to drink as much as his mother did.

### THE KIDNEY POUNDER

As she liked to call it, was inside the trailer. Technically, the pounder's called a lithotripsy machine, she said, and it delivers extracorporeal shock waves and breaks up the stones. Around the metropolitan area, and sometimes in upstate New York, she followed the trailer to cut-rate hospitals, assisting whatever doctor had been assigned to it by putting the patients onto the platform, adjusting the Velcro straps, giving her spiel about how this would hurt but not as much as passing a big stone—if it even passed—and then she'd work the device, pushing as gently as possible while the pulsing waves of ultrasonic energy broke the stone apart.

### A MALE PATIENT

Would come into the trailer, bitching and moaning, and use the occasion to touch her knee. A woman would come in, gaunt and frail, barely able to walk, resisting all help, clambering onto the platform, brushing away her offered hand.

### ALL PAIN

Seemed to be equalized as she worked the machine, pressing the device, hitting the stone hard with ultrasonic energy, until personality and differences seemed to her to be fused into a single point.

### THE SCAR

That ran down his neck—just missing his carotid artery, she noticed—and disappeared beneath his scrubs gave, when she asked him about it, an excuse to talk about the war, the time an IED hit his Hummer, blowing a tire off the vehicle, sending shrapnel through the undercarriage and into his buddy's arm. Bleeding bad, his friend screamed that he was dying, that his arm was shredded meat. But the dude's arm was perfectly fine in the end and it was only the fog-of-war shit. I guess I'm gonna live, his buddy said when he finally realized that his arm was still there, I guess I'm okay, Chief.

### KIDNEY BOY

Was this kid, barely twenty, a junkie from the looks of it, suffering for a couple of weeks while the trailer was way up north in a place called Watertown, licking a morphine lollipop, with a big stone and a tight ureter, meaning, like, the worst-case scenario: he's not only going to be pounded but it's going to take a couple of sessions and the fragments are going to pass one at a time, and then a ureteral stent will be put in, too. The kid had this crooked jaw from a bad rewire, and when I unstrapped him he kissed me and said I saved his life, said it like he meant it, and I tried not to let him see it in my eyes—you know, the things I was seeing about his future—she told Marlon one day. He leaned forward and listened to her without a word.

## DURING

Most of these breaks, the air conditioner in the trailer would pop on, devouring the sounds: the tink of a ball hitting the backstop at the schoolyard across the street, the skittering of litter in the parking lot, sirens and the deep-blue buzz of the hospital itself. When it went off, the summer would reappear, the chirping of birds and the shush of cars on the road beyond the decorative bushes.

## KIDNEY BOY

Said I'm not going to make it, and she assured him that he would but heard the truth in his voice and saw it in his eyes. You know how that is, she said. He was seeing what I saw but couldn't tell him.

## NOTHING GOOD

Could come from the intimacy of those post-treatment moments, when a patient was disoriented by a joyous sensation of relief, he thought. That was when they did weird shit, reaching out to touch you, saying something about putting you in their will, or even, in some cases, lashing out for no good reason, because you were a bearer of good tidings.

## HE RESISTED

Giving her the standard nurse-to-nurse talk about not internalizing the pain of the patients, how they come and go fleetingly. The ones you think are going to live end up dead. The ones you're sure are going to die, who have death in their eyes, end up living, processed out and sent on their merry way. Changing bedpans and lifting armrests and holding shoulders, checking charts, slipping little baggies over the tips of thermometers, inserting IV needles. Then the sensation of going outside for a break and seeing that, although inside a patient has just grunted and gone into cardiac arrest with a no-assist order, the sky, filled with clouds and sunlight and birds, is still throwing itself majestically over the world.

## SHE CRIED

About Kidney Boy, and he drew her close, giving her a chance to glance down, through the blue light of his shirt, at a switchyard of ridges where the scar opened up into the crater where the frag had gone in.

## THE TRAILER

Arrived every few weeks that summer, and they texted each other and met.

## ITINERANT LIFE

Following the trailer from one town to the next, staying in budget hotels, watching television alone in the evenings, didn't bother her much, because before Holiday Court she and her mother had traveled around a lot, following one asshole after another, and she got used to it, she said one afternoon, brushing her hair away from her forehead and looking out over the bushes to the kids playing on the ball field across the street and then, turning around quickly, gazing over his shoulder at the hill that climbed past the road in the other direction, across the parking lot, where tombstones rose up into the trees. It seemed pretty typical, putting a graveyard next to a hospital.

## THE DEAD

Had names that stuck in the mind, whereas those of the ones who were cured were released, sent back into the clean, raw rotation of the stars, so to speak, he said. There was always some patient in critical condition, doomed and marked terminal on the charts, who overcame the odds and marched out of the ward surrounded by his family, not even waving goodbye, taking a name off into the future.

## MARLON

Liked her white arms, and the way her breasts swayed beneath the fabric of her scrubs, and he thought—when she and the trailer were gone—about the way her ass shifted when she walked, throwing a compaction from one side to the other, revealing to him a complication of form that begged to be touched, giving him, during lonely nights in his shitty apartment, something to imagine: falling to his knees and extending his arms out like one of those mythic figures offering a baby to the sun or to God, gently cradling each side of her beautiful bottom.

### GRACIE

Admired the bulk of his body and his dark skin and his muscular heft in combination with the way he shifted from foot to foot when he was standing and the way, when he was on the curb smoking, he looked beyond her to some point on the horizon that nobody could see, pulling his long black hair tighter into the regulation ponytail, holding his head high and working his jaw as he talked, letting his upstate intonations enter his voice, and the way he assumed a weird, regal formality, stopping to bow to her as he emerged from the emergency-room doors, sweeping his arm out to the side, looking grim and lonely until he unleashed his smile in a way that seemed vulnerable and tough all at the same time.

### SHOSHONE

Folk loved the wolf, he told her one afternoon when she asked him about life in Ely, Nevada. Wolf could bring people back to life but he didn't do it, because there'd be too many people in the world if he did. I'm not sure how the story goes, but it's something like that, he said, and it was about the only thing my mother ever really told me about our people.

## TWO NURSES, SMOKING

### HALF-HOUR

Breaks adding up, one after another, over four months.

### THE LONELIEST ROAD

In America is Route 50 in Nevada, and it goes through Ely.
Driving it's like losing your soul and getting another one, my
mom used to say. My father drove out 50 and disappeared
for a year and came back saying that he'd never got off it—
the road, I mean—and then she left him, or he left her, or
they left each other. I've got fifty versions of that story. Another thing she told me was that folks in San Francisco said
they had to drive east to get to the west. She had this hang-
up about being from the west, and then there she was, living
in Newburgh, New York.

### RIFFING

About the serial-killer nurse, expounding on something
he'd read online about this male nurse who admitted to
killing patients, mostly in Pennsylvania, adjusting morphine drips and rewriting charts, covering his tracks. By
that point she had given him the entire Kidney Boy story,
how she'd seen in his eyes that he would commit suicide,
even the fact that he'd throw himself from a bridge. A few
days later, he told one about his buddy who was killed in
Iraq. Same old story, IED, blasting up through the undercarriage, tearing a hole and all of that, except this time it

wasn't his arm but his head and upper torso, and the light went out of his eyes.

## PLAY IT OUT

She was saying. He was hunching his shoulders, his face buried in his hands. The way I see it, that serial-killer nurse isn't a real killer; he can take or leave the death part, because what he really likes is scoping out the possibilities—you know the ones I'm talking about, the pre-op patients who want you to lend an ear so they can decide that you're gonna be a good-luck charm, taking your hand and complimenting your nursing skills, understanding full well the implications of the coming surgery, whatever. You go in and for a minute, even if you try not to, you feel the life in your hand and you become aware that one little fuckup on a chart, or a misreading, and the patient could die. Or when you go in to find balloons and cards tacked to a board and see some little kid—always named Sammy or Annie—with a shaved head and pre-surgery marks and you think, against your will, how fucking easy it would be to save the kid from suffering, he said, looking out over the road, streaming his smoke between his teeth, with his eyes on the horizon and his chin jutting.

## ON THE STEPS

Of the trailer a few days later, picking up on the subject of the serial-killer nurse, he began to talk again about the impulse to kill, how he'd learned in Fallujah that impulse equals mess, and how there was a guy in the unit who plugged shots whenever he saw fit, and one day some old lady came around the corner with her hand in the air—we hated corners, he said, which was one reason we hated Fallujah—and this guy in our unit just popped her. When we got close to the body, we saw that she had these arthritic hands, fingers curled, so a hand held up like that might've looked like a gun. But it was really just sloppy shit, the truth.

## BEAUTIFUL

Inside that moment—his voice quivering, his eyes welling— the wind was rising and the darker clouds were coming in. His eyes were painfully green as the grief twisted his face and the trees near the road gave off a sugary odor and tenderness formed in the quiet. How long was that moment, held in memory between the two of them for the rest of their lives?

## FINALLY

He spoke and said, My grandmother had rheumatoid arthritis, and I used to go with her to Ely, to this clinic where she put her hands into a wax bath while I watched, dipping them in and wincing, at first, until she had blue wax gloves. Then he shook a cigarette from his pack and lit up, and they sat and listened to the sounds of summer, looking over the bushes at the baseball diamond and, beyond it, at the top of the school and the white cupola in the sky. When he spoke again, he explained that the dead lady on the street in Fallujah had had hands just like his grandmother's, and then he began to cry, starting with a single low gasp and a collapse of his shoulders as he buried his face, and she pulled him close.

## ONE

Hopes for the great love born of a common pain, for two united souls sharing grief in long, easy banter while they fend off physical attraction and misread each other until everything seems to change one afternoon, smoking behind the trailer on a particularly rough day—a triaged bus accident that included one double amputee, a burn victim (for him), and (for her) a woman who came in with a story to tell about her previous stones and a time when she was so bad, lying on her side in her living room, bucking in agony, that she begged her husband to kick her, and he did just that, walloping her, and her husband was arrested, of course, but it worked, and the stone passed in her piss. The cops wouldn't listen to her side of the story, though, and her husband ended up in jail. Damn right, Marlon said—and then, just after she finished that story, there was the whoop of a siren and an EMS pulled in and they watched while overhead, from a thin stack on the roof of the hospital, a bloom of smoke emerged into the early autumnal sky, the incinerated aftermath of old bandages and bloodied towels, afterbirths, and whatever else could be burned to save the hospital disposal fees.

## ONE AFTERNOON IN SEPTEMBER

He said, I love hearing your stories. I love your stories, too, she said, touching his shoulder.

## TWO NURSES, SMOKING

### WE SHOULD GET OUT OF HERE

After this shift, take a drive, he said, shrugging his shoulder toward the emergency entrance, where the orderlies were removing a gurney from a truck, lowering it with a count. And she waited to answer, because she wanted him to beg a little, to hear how much his desire had accrued over the weeks—small hand brushes and gestures, one to the next— and because she took care with matters of the heart, the past having taught her that a hit could come as easily as a kiss.

### THEY DROVE

Up the old state road through autumn dusk, talking softly and listening to music as the river appeared and disappeared to the right and she fiddled with the old-radio punch buttons, feeling the mechanism moving the pointer as it slid from station to station.

### THEY BOTH FELT

The sensation of going north, while he told stories about growing up, the gangs that ruled the neighborhood, the way they used to play along the river, and then, around the switchbacks of Storm King and passing through the desolation of Newburgh, he said, I think this here is probably the loneliest road in America, and they headed out of town, continuing north as the road opened into four lanes and then back to two, skirting old estates and monasteries, until they reached a small hotel up on a berm on the left, painted pink, with a quivering neon sign that said RIVER REST, something from an old movie.

NO

Wait, before they got to the hotel they stopped at a diner, sharing a meal, and then in the parking lot they smoked and leaned back, gazing up at the stars—and if you'd been looking you would have seen them there and speculated on two people lingering in an upstate parking lot, kissing each other gently, and you would've extrapolated a story from that image.

NO

Wait, there were a lot of other conversations, late in the summer and early in the fall, as they stared out at the road and the ball field and the sky, testing each other, teasing, griping about work and life in general, sharing deeper stories that'll never be recorded, not here, and not in memory, so that later, looking back, it would seem that in the fall, on a cold afternoon, they had both decided on a whim to take the leap, to hook up, to go into the future together, to consummate the hesitant, careful nature of their personalities, because they were both damaged, somehow lost, and sensed and felt—you'd see if you'd been watching—a suddenly deep need for each other.

NO

Wait, go back to the afternoon she told him the Kidney Boy story, to the way that exchange had worked temporally, the things that were withheld and the things that were expressed, the way she told Marlon how she imagined the kid, whose name was Curt, going up to the bridge, standing on the railing, and looking straight ahead—at the bend in the river, the beautiful vista. Go back to the way the exchange transpired— almost wordlessly, but not quite—that afternoon between Marlon and Gracie, and how he said "of course," after she told him Kidney Boy's real name, Curt, and then he laughed and said, All those stoners have short names, like Hank, Curt, Al. How after she'd talked about the broken jaw she abruptly changed the subject to something her dentist had told her about boys (she said boys) coming into the office on Sunday afternoons with bar-fight jaws, broken teeth. Go back to how, after she'd told Marlon about the dentist, an old couple appeared between the sliding doors and began a slow, shuffling walk across the parking lot, holding each other up, and how he paused (holding off on the nursing lecture) and said, How did Curt die? He said it before she could tell him the fact. Not so much guessing as seeming to have a prophetic insight. And she said, Hey, how'd you know?, and he shrugged and looked away and listened as she explained that Curt had jumped from a bridge, and then, right then, the wind lifted and litter skittered and an EMS came into the emergency bay and across the street there was the high, metallic, and beautiful sound of kids playing before she began to cry.

NO

Wait, go back to the way he emerged from the sliding glass doors in his army fatigues over his scrubs with his hood

pulled up around a face grimly set, his small mouth puckered, as if he were deep in thought, until he got near the
trailer and pulled his hood down and shook his head to
let his hair out and paused for a moment, extending his
arms as if for an embrace, and then said, Heyya, heyya, and
gave her a hug while she held the story she wanted to tell
him about the crazy old lady up in Poughkeepsie, because
she always had one bottled up, at bay, and that was part of
the dynamic, the urge to talk to him, and to hear him talk
back.

**NO**

Wait, go back behind the trailer, to that particularly rough
day, a triaged bus accident, two DOA and one double
amputee, for him, and for her an old man with a stone the
size of the Hope Diamond in for the second time, and the
lady who argued over her technique with the pounder,
giving her grief, and to make up for it decided to tell Gracie her life story, ten stones in five years—was what she
said—and a slow passer, taking her time, a regular at the
hospital. And then Gracie told Marlon about her mom,
about the way her stepfather had beaten them both, and
then about Roy, the guy at Holiday Court, this wiry older
guy—at least he seemed older to me at the time, she said—
who had a motorcycle and took her for rides, and then she
stopped speaking and let Marlon see in her face the things
she wanted him to see, that she had suffered at the hands
of Roy.

NO

Wait, go to the moment when suddenly, out of the blue, a freak snow squall had appeared from a cloudless sky, and he said it was a good omen, and she told him he was full of shit, and they fell into a hysterical laughing fit together as, once again, an EMS came roaring in—siren whooping—as if to counterpoint their joy and delight with the urgency of some other realm, and how that moment, amid the countless others, somehow sealed a fate between them within the shared eternity of those moments.

NO

Wait, go back to that afternoon, when he said, We should get out of this place, or perhaps he said, We should get away from this joint, and shrugged a shoulder back toward the emergency entrance, where—with a clank-and-clattering sound—they were removing a gurney from the truck, lowering it on a count, which was a sign of something horrible, because they only did that for the messed-up cases, the damaged goods, and she waited a few beats to answer Marlon, because she wanted him to say it again, to beg a little bit, to see just how much desire had accrued over the weeks, from one small hand brush to another, from one gesture to the next, because that was all she had in the end: all she had— she sometimes felt—was the small accumulations, one upon the next, because the past had taught her to take care with all of that, to be frugal with matters of the heart. A hit could come as easily as a kiss. The back of a hand could arrive at a moment's notice. This physics was in her bones, in the way she drew herself slightly away, even now, when he reached out to touch her shoulder. She felt herself—with the breeze blowing her hair around her eyes—withdrawing a little bit from the pliant urgency in his voice when he told her that he just felt like getting away. So she waited until he added, I'm not hitting on you, I'm just proposing a drive up the river, and then they both laughed at that. And she waited a few more beats, and then said, Sure, which was, he thought, the most beautiful word in the world.

## SO

Now they were in a bed, in the shadowy hotel light, listening to the occasional car passing on the road.

## IN THE SAGGING BED

He heaved into her, lifting himself up on his hands, while she held his shoulders, her fingers sliding around to feel the scar coming down from his neck and channeling out in two lines that then met again around his left nipple to form a craterlike hollow, and she drew on her time in nursing school, testing the tissue where the shrapnel went in and stayed in and burned—he'd later say—phosphorous white and hot enough, thank God, to cauterize the wound and seal off the blood vessels. He thrust down and deep and then eased up as she pushed against him—forgetting his scars—until the two motions spun into what seemed to be an airless freedom. He grunted, and she came, too, her finger flicking.

## A SOFT WEEPING

Sound—as close to crying as you could get—and when she made that sound he made it, too, and together they were making one sound, and then he rested his weight against her and recalled her hand down there, fluttering, reminding him of the old woman's hand and of his grandmother's, too, because to touch herself she'd had to bend and flex it, and remembering the feeling after the fact, he felt sure that he would tell her what had really happened to the old lady in Fallujah, or at least later—much later, years later—he'd see that image and use it to justify having told her about it.

## DEEP IN THE NIGHT

He nudged her awake and explained that he was the one who'd gone trigger-happy on the old lady in Fallujah, shooting her on raw impulse instead of thought as she came around the corner, taking her out from twenty yards away.

## HE CRIED

Against her shoulder as she said, softly, It's all right, Marlon, you're here now and it's going to work out, you're a damn good nurse, and then it seemed as if all she had ever learned on the job came into play as she spoke soothingly to him, making a gentle patting motion on his back, the kind of gesture you'd use to calm a baby at night—a gentle repeated pat, not too soft and not too hard.

## SO THAT

The deepest enigmatic meaning would seem to stay around that image, not just of the two of them crying together but also of the hand itself, as it fluttered alone, which had led to his admission, and for her that image would hold another meaning, because she would remember it, too, vaguely, and replicate the motion countless times over the years, giving herself pleasure, just as she'd often backtrack through her memory of that summer and fall, drawing on the random moments, trying to find the origin point of their love.

# VOWS

never caught exactly what was said about us and could only imagine the vicious forms the rumor took as it started at the church and jumped from house to house along the river, somehow making the two-mile leap over Tallman Mountain State Park as it headed to the town of Piermont, where the Dickersons lived, and then from Jenny Dickerson's mouth up the river several blocks, skipping the Morrison house (she was rarely home), most likely to Sue Carson, and then from her mouth to Andrew Jensen, the rector at St. Anne's, who, I still liked to imagine, spiced the rumor with some biblical flavor, somehow couching his comments in theological terms, mentioning the fall and temptation and the sins of adultery and so on and so on as he passed it to Gracie Gray, who tasted all the possible rami-fications, twisted it even more to make me into a villainous antihero, unaware that both of us, Sharon and I, had betrayed each other, and then held the story in her mouth for several weeks, where it sat until I turned from the window at our annual holiday cocktail party to find her looking at me.

In a teal dress, tailored square to her shoulders, cut low in a rectangle, framing pale flesh and her pearls, which swayed as she moved gently to the music, Gracie winked at me and then turned away coyly, rotating at the waist and letting her legs—I swear I remember this!—swing around in an afterthought, as if she were resisting a magnetic pull. Then, in exactly the same way, she slowly turned back and reconnected with my gaze and, while the midnight cold from the window behind me brushed my neck, we seemed at that instant to share an exchange.

Her side of the exchange seemed to be saying: *In your public retaking of vows a few months ago, you and Sharon exposed a crack in the facade—the happy couple! Ha! The perfectly wonderful family!—and although that crack has been sealed in a ceremony with new vows, it remains a crack.*

While my part of the exchange went: *I understand that you think the seal might still be weak, Gracie, but it's not, not anymore.*

Then she squinted her eyes at me and gave me a look that seemed to say: *Don't flatter yourself, jerk. You're a creep. I'm simply offering you a little holiday gesture of flirtatious cheer to warm your lonely, pathetic soul, and, anyway, after hearing the rumor, and then passing it on to Stacy Sutton, telling her how you betrayed Sharon, I'll be the first one to pry you two apart, to weaken the seal. On the other hand*—she widened her eyes and then winked—*perhaps sometime in the future on a night like this—crisp and clear outside, with an almost artificial-looking*

*rime of frost in the corners of each windowpane—with all of this*
*good fortune in the air, well, who knows? Is there anything more*
*dangerous than a full-blown sense of good fortune?*

Looking back, I think that we might've had a similar
exchange—if you want to call it that—at the church, after
Sharon and I kissed, as I swept the sanctuary from pew to
pew to make sure everyone got a chance to witness the
frankness in my face, because after we sealed our new commitment with a kiss I got a sense in the late-day light trying
to come through the stained glass overhead, in the big brass
cross behind me, in the way it felt to stand on the altar, that
Sharon and I were being held up to a judgment that hadn't
existed before the ceremony.

Before the renewal ceremony began there had been a
new sense of mission between us, an eagerness that had disappeared as soon as we started reciting our vows. When we
turned to each other, with Reverend Woo between us, and
began speaking, it was in the subdued, somewhat feverous
voices of two people who had reconciled after one final,
devastating argument that had lasted several months, beginning one day at the beach in Mystic, Connecticut, with the
Thompsons, who were down near the water when I turned
to Sharon and said, All this pain will pass. We really can work
this out.

And she said, I no longer care what Dr. Haywood says.
The middle ground doesn't seem to be available for us.

And I said, quoting Dr. Haywood again, Gunner must be

kept front and center. It's our duty to him to do everything we can to build a new life out of the ruins.

Down the sand, Gunner yelled, What did you say about me? Hey, hey, you guys, what are you talking about?

Sharon's face was soft, lovely, tan. Her eyes were pooling a sadness that I found attractive. Near the water, Carol Thompson, who at that time didn't have the slightest idea what was going on, was lifting her son up by the hands, swaying him over the water and dipping his toes into the surf.

Her husband, Ron, was a few yards down the beach, holding himself at a remove, shielding his brow as he serenely scanned the water. For a few seconds there was a shift in the air, Sharon was gazing out at the water and we both felt a stasis, a place where we could rebuild our marriage, and then the feeling disappeared—and Gunner called again, waving his blue shovel—and she leaned in and whispered, Fuck you, and I whispered, No, fuck you, and then I lay on my side and watched out of the corner of my eye as Carol lifted her son up and down (she had strong shoulders and long, elegant arms, and I felt, watching her, with the sand against my legs, the soft seep of ardor coming again).

*Ardor* was a word I used a lot back then when I talked to myself. Ardor's taking over, I said. The air is loaded with ardor this afternoon, I said to Gunner as I watched him, day after day, in the backyard. Ardor's radiating from those trees, I said in a mock-British accent, pointing at the pines along the edge of the yard. Then he scrunched his face and gave me a look that said: *You're strange and silly, Dad. Whatever you're saying, it's dubious.*

His look seemed judgmental in the purest sense, as if he

knew somehow that his mother and father had betrayed each other, parted ways, heading off into distant blissful worlds.

On the beach that day in Mystic I rolled over and kept my face down and admitted to myself, as I do now, that it had been in the end inevitable, considering the amount of ardor—or ardor-related gestures generated—that the lust, or whatever, would congeal, or perhaps the word I want is *incarnate*, into an act of adultery on my part and, at almost the same time, on Sharon's part.

Sharon had confessed to me about her lover, the Banker, and I had confessed to her about Marie, whom she called the Teacher, and in those confessions we had each allowed carefully curated details in—the Standard Hotel on Washington Street, a few drinks after a long session briefing a client, a clandestine meeting in Piermont on a lonely, sad day in the fall when she was out in Los Angeles, time zones away. A Lorca poem memorized in Spanish. Funds transferred into an account managed by the Banker. The rest was left up to our horrific imaginations. I imagined her eating lunch with him, down the stairs in one of those older Upper East Side establishments, with ivory-white tablecloths and candles flickering in the middle of the day. Outside the windows, I imagined the legs and high heels and shoes of those walking past while they whispered sweet nothings to each other, and felt the beautiful, clandestine joy of holding a secret together in Manhattan. What she imagined I can only imagine, but I'm sure she built images of me with Marie, images of her face drawn from parent-teacher

conferences: the two of us leaning back on a blanket somewhere deep in the state park, looking up at the sky, smiling
in postcoital quiet, watching the clouds meander over the
river. I imagined that she imagined—as I did—lips hovering, dappled with sweat, just before a kiss. The faint, citrusy
smell of her neck. The sweet moments between touch—a
finger hovering just over the flesh. Exquisite pain, of course,
came from these imagined moments because they were
pure, clear, drawn from the mind's own unique desires.

At the beach that day in Mystic, with my cheek against
the sand, I felt a keen injustice in the clichéd nature of our
situation, that thinking it was a cliché was also a cliché, or
maybe bringing it up as a cliché is even more of a cliché,
and even more of a cliché to bring up the fact that a cliché is
a cliché.

What are clichés but the reduction of experience into
manageable patterns, Dr. Haywood told us a few weeks
later, during a counseling session. You call it a cliché, but the
brain can only process so much.

That day in her office—on the ground floor of an apartment building on Ninety-sixth Street, not far from the
park—Dr. Haywood explained that the brain's attention
can be drawn precisely to only one thing at a time, and only
those things the brain deems worthy. You catch a flick of
movement in the grass, near the water's edge, and then you
draw your attention to it if you deem it worthy, or else you
let it float away and think: *That's just a bird alighting, or flying*
*off, and I'm going to keep my attention on that boat, the leader of*
*a regatta, tacking around a buoy, catching the wind in the belly of a*

*sail.* Cliché, she explained, is the brain's way of speeding up cognitive analysis.

I lifted myself up and brushed the sand from my arms and leaned toward Sharon and said, Well, Sharon, we need to go back to our original vows and start from scratch, and she said, Honestly, I'm sorry to say, but in retrospect the original vows didn't cut it in the first place. The original vows were obviously batshit silly.

She kept talking until Gunner came up along the sand, walking with his side-to-side sway, looking suspicious. For several days he'd been listening carefully as we spoke in a weird manner, keeping everything—as far as we could—cryptic.

Betrayal doesn't go away, Sharon said.

I'd like to find a firm footing. Something we can stand on.

What are you talkin' about? Gunner said. What about my foot?

Mom and Daddy are talking adult talk. Sometimes adults have to talk adult talk, Sharon said.

Then he began to pressure and pry and make us both deeply uncomfortable but also—it seems to me now, sitting here alone with my drink, watching the water—even more eager to find a language that might, without exposing our plight, also prove magically useful. We had to blur the details and speak in code and we ended up speaking in a kind of neo-biblical lingo.

I'm not sure we can make it up this hill.

The hill is made of your frickin' ardor.

No, no, the hill is a big-shot banker in Manhattan. We both climbed hills. We're both equally guilty.

What hill can't be climbed? I want to climb the hill with you, Gunner said, and in between our words there would appear a hint of solace, of the reconciliation that would arrive if we simply continued speaking in code for the rest of our lives with our son between us, asking suspicious questions, redirecting our pain into his pale blue eyes, his tiny ears.

Anthony's Nose, one of us said, referring to the beautiful mountain east of the Bear Mountain Bridge. We're talking about taking a climb up Anthony's Nose.

I wanna climb the nose, Gunner said. His eyes were wide and resolute and sparked—it seemed—with a keen knowingness, a sense of playful desperation.

That afternoon with the Thompsons on the beach in Mystic, we began an argument that continued into fall, taking any number of forms: me in support of the original vows; Sharon against; vows dead and dried up and scattered forever in the dusty winds of our infidelity. Vows broken to begin with, tried, simplistic and never powerful enough to determine our future; vows subsumed under the weight of dead traditions, symbolic claptrap uttered from youthful throats that had been eager, ready to say anything (any fucking thing, Sharon cried) in order to instill a sense of permanency in the world. We fought and eventually—in that strange way that one argument can lead to another and then to something that resembles silence—we reached the end point, at which action is the only recourse.

But before we got to that point we had to go through

a fight that night, after our trip to the beach, with our skin still salty and taut and Gunner asleep in front of the television set. While I argued in support of our original vows, taken years ago on a crisp, clear fall afternoon in the city, Sharon made the case—her voice deepening, shifting into her attorney mode—that those vows were dead and gone, used up, depleted, scattered forever on the cold wind of our infidelity.

A week later, at the top of Anthony's Nose, keeping Gunner close at hand, standing there with her hands on her hips and her chin up as if speaking to the sky, she explained that she thought our commitment had been flawed anyway, silly and traditional. We were just kids. We didn't know what we were doing.

On Anthony's Nose we were rehashing previous fights, looking down at the river where it went north past West Point, buried in the haze.

Sharon pointed out, her voice getting soft and gentle, that we had never really discussed ("had a sit-down" was the phrase she used) the wording of those original vows and had instead entrusted their composition to Reverend Moody (Judson Church in Washington Square), the same man who had married her parents back in Cleveland. We had seen him as a kind of good-luck token, because his words had sealed the covenant—I remember she argued that that was a much better word—that had led to her conception and then her existence and, via her existence, to our meeting by pure chance that day on the Boston Common, sitting on the same bench and reading the same book (*Pale Fire* by Vladimir Nabokov).

We bickered and fought and then finally renewed our vows at the little Presbyterian church in Snedens Landing, New York, about twenty miles north of Manhattan, on the west side of the river, tucked amid expensive estates—Baryshnikov lived back there, along with Bill Murray.

The Reverend Woo presided, leaning forward in her vestments, quoting Merton on humility (my contribution) and Robert Frost on roads not taken (Sharon's contribution), while Gracie Gray, John and Sue Carson, Joanna and Bill and Jenny Dickerson, Bill and Liz Wall, Karen Drake and Janet Smith, Jillian and Ted Wilson-Rothchild, and Sharon's mother, Anna Rose, who had flown over from Tralee, Ireland, looked on as I repeated Woo's words back to Sharon—*For eternity, ever after, we renew these vows in the great spiral of time itself, the dark matter of our particular, unique love, tucked in the folds of the universe, marking our small minutia of time here out of the random chaos, uniting our love to a semblance of form, tightening ourselves against the timescape of our lives*—until it was my turn to listen to Woo speak Sharon's part of the vows, and I tried to stay focused as she recited her part back to me, something about *the renewal of the original impulse of our love, returning to the original pulse of desire that is on this day consecrated* (I'm pretty sure she spoke both those phrases: "the original impulse" and then "on this day consecrated").

Her side mentioned Gunner—something along the lines of *between us, shared, our devout love of our son, Gunner, stands.*

She listened to Woo speak a few words and then to me as I repeated those words, and then I listened to Woo speak

and then to Sharon again, and then we kissed each other
with honest eagerness and stood arm in arm while out in
the pews, next to Sharon's mother, who was dressed in a
lime-green blouse and a pleated herringbone skirt, looking weary and jet-lagged after her flight across the Atlantic,
Gunner stared at me with blunt blue eyes that seemed to
say: *You have betrayed me, Father, insofar as you had a part in my
creation.*

Please don't think I'm trying to say, as I sit here alone enjoying the warm summer evening, alone in the house, and once
again, for perhaps the thousandth time, studying the Hudson
River, that we didn't renew our commitment with the most
devout sincerity, or that retaking our vows wasn't the right
thing to do at the time, or that it wasn't a pleasure to leave
Gunner with Sharon's mother and drive away from the front
of the church, in the verdant spring air, trailing a ridiculous
string of rattling cans all the way through Queens to the
long-term parking at JFK. But the look my son gave me, or
at least the look I imagined he gave me, seemed to reveal
that even he was aware that the renewal ceremony revealed,
or rather exposed, a rending to our friends, to the public, to
the world at large.

Please, will you stop about the look Gunner gave you,
Sharon said that night in Dublin. You're being ridiculous.
He has no idea. If anything, he's happy for us.
    She was at the window of our room in the Gresham

Hotel, her back turned to me, looking down at O'Connell Street. It was a lovely evening with a breeze blowing through the window, brushing her hair around her shoulders. (Oh God, Sharon had the most beautiful auburn hair with natural highlights! And, oh, those eyes, mercurial, quicksilver eyes that shifted with mood and light! Even now I can recall the look she had given me earlier that day as we stood on a bridge and looked down at the Liffey—solemn and dark water below, which seemed to hold centuries of stonework and old barges and history going back to the Vikings, coming back up into her eyes as she gave me one of her sidelong glances, flirtatious and judgmental at the same time, and then she gave me her wonderful smile.)

At the window with her hands on her hips she was swaying gently, shifting her weight from one foot to the other. Come to bed, I said. I won't ever say that word again. It doesn't need to be said. I promise.

What word?

*Vows*, I said.

Oh, honestly, I said I don't want to hear that word ever again.

I stayed silent as we lay together in bed. We had walked aimlessly to stay awake, to fight off the jet lag, drinking coffee, surprised at the clean modernity of the city, arm in arm as we stood at the Trinity gate, which was closed, and then strolled down Grafton Street—like any mall in America, we agreed—to St. Stephen's Green, where we found a bench and sat for a while and held hands like proper newlyweds. Then, as we meandered back in the direction of the hotel, we lucked upon Oscar Wilde's house, or at least I insisted, before we crossed the street, that it was Wilde's house. In reality it was his father's house. The confusion sparked a short, brisk argument—the first of our renewed marriage!—as we waited for the light to change. Sharon's voice had tightened and became litigious, resolute and pristine in a way I admired and loved. The argument began on one side of the street and ended when we got close enough to read the round plaque that described an eye surgeon and folklore expert, Wilde's father.

You were right, I told Sharon, feeling incredibly happy.

Then we made our way back down O'Connell Street, stopping here and there to look at the shops, laughing and teasing each other about Oscar Wilde, and we ended up at the bar in the touristy pub next to the hotel, sitting shoulder to shoulder, still weary from jet lag, leaning like regulars into our pints and sipping together in unison, sharing for the first time a mutual loneliness (a kind of blissful isolation, a sense that we were united in our new bonds) that would—I now see—last for years, until we held hands in the hospital room and prayed softly together while outside the sky over the river charged up with particles and produced, somewhere over New Jersey, a bright flash of lightning.

Was it a cliché to have a second honeymoon in Ireland? Sure. Is it a cliché to link that one drink together in the pub, after our first fight at Oscar Wilde's father's house, with our relationship after our renewal ceremony? Is it a cliché to make the leap from that moment—when we were first feeling the deep unity between us that would last for years and years—to that final night in the hospital along the upper western edge of Manhattan, when I held her hand and felt the faint bud of pulse in her wrist and then pulled her hand to my mouth and began to weep?

Yes, perhaps. But what Haywood said to us that day in therapy stuck. To push further, as I sit here today I am sure that in the hospital—with blue sawhorses in the street set up by the police, and a summer thunderstorm brewing over Jersey—with our hands cupped gently, we both felt the beauty of our commitment to time itself, to something vast and eternal and, above all, secretive. It was ours and ours alone. Whatever rumors and hearsay and conjecture floated around our story, whatever people made of it from gathered fragments, could only intensify what we had together.

On a family trip out west years after the ceremony, watching the road taper into the horizon outside of Bismarck, North Dakota, I began to wonder if we had completely nullified each other's vows by renewing them. I theorized that Sharon's vows had simply canceled mine out, creating a different kind of void. Gunner was sixteen at the time, lurking in the back seat with his headphones on, and the sight of his bobbing head, with a halo of hair puffing around his headphone band in the rearview mirror, had been disconcerting. Looking drunk back there, with his eyes loose and formless, lost in his music, he could've been anywhere.

Next to me, Sharon slept with her head back and her mouth open. That's what I recall from our Grand Canyon trip. Sharon sleeping and my son, with his adult bones eagerly hardening beneath his muscles and his muscles pushing against the fabric of his sleeves, in the back seat, lost in his beloved death metal. Even at the rim of the canyon, looking down, taking in the vast expanse, all he did was nod his head slightly to the music in his headphones and casually brush off the sublime vista.

On the way home, I think, this theory of a complete nullification of vows came to mind.

As I drove, I balled the thought up—the theory of complete nullification—and threw it out the window. That's a meditation technique I was using at the time: take a thought, write it down on some mental paper, hold it, turn it around in the mind, center on it, and then ball it up and throw it away.

Somewhere along a road in North Dakota, I tossed that thought out the window.

Now, sitting here, I imagine it's still out there, curled in the scrub and dust, waiting to be discovered and unfolded.

One night, standing over my son as he slept, while the snow swirled around outside, it struck me that if we ever had another renewal ceremony, a kind of third-time-is-a-charm deal, we'd have to simply act as our own authority before God and avoid all the formal trappings. (Those are the fun parts, Sharon said, her voice light and happy, when we were planning the second ceremony. The trappings are the part you're required to forget the first time you get married. We were too young, and uptight, and we forgot them. The point of a renewal ceremony is to have a deeper awareness and enjoyment and focus so you actually experience the trappings, she said. I said, I don't like the trappings, but you might be right. You've got to have some kind of sacred space overhead, some sense that the vows are being taken in a holy environment. Even if you get married on the beach, there has to be a consecrated vibe in the air, and she said, Yeah, right, with an edge to her voice, not bitter but not sweet.)

Sharon and I are still uncomfortable with each other, I told my friend Ted one afternoon, before the renewal ceremony. We were out on the back patio, smoking cigars, facing the river. As the sun came in and out of the clouds, the trees blazed with color and faded and blazed.

We're like a couple of crooks locked in a cell with a warden who looms over us to make sure we get along for eternity. We're both in for the death penalty, I said.

You're in for death, and so am I. Each meal is a last supper, he said, and we laughed. He and his wife were astonishingly good cooks, master chefs, and their dinner parties were legendary. They weren't foodies. Their respect for food went beyond trends or fads. They cooked simple, elegant meals and knew how to set up a perfect party. Brisk fall nights with a hint of wood smoke and harvest in the air. The windows of their house above the road, tucked in a notch in the palisade, flickering candlelight. Silver on white linen. Always perfectly balanced company, a few lighthearted guests, a sullen guest (Hal Jacobson, whose wife had jumped from the bridge), a blend of intellect, jest, and despair brought together, drawn around a sense that the next dish would top the last, bringing all attention to the mouth and tongue.

No matter what was being said, no matter how happy the talk, no matter what grievances were exposed, the next dish brought the conversation to a satisfying lull.

Before the dish arrived, we'd be complaining about the town's new sidewalk design, or someone would bring up the so-called nunnery that was, at that time, proposed for the empty meadow lot up near Hook Mountain. (I would keep quiet about the fact that I owned the small parcel that was necessary for an easement. It would come out soon enough. One way or another, if the proposal moved forward and went through the planning-board review process, the need for an easement would come to light and, with it, the fact that I owned the land. Then the fact that the New York diocese was negotiating with me to purchase it would come out, too.)

I'm only kidding about prison, I said to Ted, who looked at me, took a deep draw, and released a cloud of smoke.

Ted was a federal judge and played the role even when he was off the bench, relaxing with a cigar in hand. He was the type who prepared his cigar in an old style, popping a nub out of the end of the cigar with his thumbnail, rejecting my clippers and then my expensive butane lighter—the flame powerful and invisible until it hit the tobacco and bloomed like a blue orchid—in favor of kitchen matches. Even when he was relaxed, he seemed to have the straight-backed reserve of a man who was withholding judgment, sticking with procedure. He took another draw on his cigar, kept his lips lightly around the wrapper leaf, and spoke with firm authority, You're not in prison. If you had a chance to ride the blue bus and then went through the security check at Rikers Island, you'd understand what it means to be in prison. But I get your point, he said.

Well, you should, I said. I knew he had gone through some serious marital problems of his own. On the porch—this was late fall, a cold wind coming from the north, hunched in our coats with our collars up, enjoying the feeling of smoking outside, as if we were in the Klondike, two rugged explorers stopping for a smoke—he knew and I knew at that instant, sitting there, that the next thing out of his mouth—or mine—would be a comment about the quality of the cigars, and then one of us would say something about the quality of the Cubans, and then one of us would tell a smuggling story. His that day was about how he once hid cigars—purchased in Europe—in his wife's tampon box to get them through customs, and I told him about replacing the bands, transforming Montecristos into Dunhills, something like that, and then we settled into a deep ritual that betrayed time itself, turning the moment into something utterly simple and meaningless.

Years later, at his funeral, up on the hill across from the hospital, with the river broken into gray slates through the trees, I'd remember that moment on the back patio and how he drew the attention away from my failure and allowed us to go back to the ordained pattern of our friendship, which had started with our weekly tennis matches. You want to play with a judge? I know this judge, and he's pretty good, someone told me. He's federal so he pretty much sets his own hours and can play with you in the afternoon, someone said.

In the years after the renewal ceremony the judge came

to know the full story of my marital problems with Sharon. His son was at West Point for a few years, and I remember that he talked often of him, saying things like, My son is a plebe, and right now, as we play tennis, he is, most certainly, being tortured into adulthood. His son would become a captain and die in his second tour in Iraq, killed by an IED, but of course we didn't know that at the time.

On the night of the party, months after the ceremony, Ted's loss of his son in Iraq was five years away, still up in the vapors, and he had no idea that it was ahead of him, and I had no idea that someday I'd look back and see both of us as we'd be years later and filter our friendship through that particular moment. Dare I say that as I turned and had that exchange with Gracie, and the judge glanced at me, we both sensed that in the future we'd look back at that moment? Ted's face, as he held the cocktail shaker in his hands, had the placid look of authority, a look I had seen after one of his fantastic tennis serves, standing with his legs apart and his racket at his side, gazing over the net with honest humility. The ball had zipped past. The air was brighter, cooler on his side of the net and duller on my side. All of his efforts— the toss-up, perfectly placed, his racket going back to touch the crook of his massive back, his swing down to meet the ball—were gone, lost, and the serve manifested itself in the tink of the ball against the chain-link behind me and then disappeared into silence as it sat alone in the corner, nestled in leaves. That was the look he had when he turned to see me at the window, at our annual party, years ago.

Then he came over to where I was standing by the window and asked if I was okay. He put his hand on my shoulder and was leaning forward and his face seemed to be saying: *Yes, I'm holding you in judgment, old friend. I'll give you my verdict in a few years.*

True love is, when seen from afar, a big fat cliché. It is a glance from the side while looking down at deep water. A fight on a beach. A sweaty brow covered with sand. Lips between kisses. Betrayal eased into grace.

(Let it go, Sharon said. You theorize too much about these things. How many times have I heard a witness claim that they told themselves to remember what they were seeing when the truth is they were too freaked out, or too scared, or even, in some cases, unaware that a crime was transpiring.)

All I can say now is that I stuck to my word. I don't think we ever discussed our vows again. We settled into life. We shared everything together. After that night in the Gresham Hotel, we went on finding places, situations, where we could simply sit side by side, shoulder to shoulder, lifting a glass in unison.

One evening, years later, we walked down Lexington Avenue after dinner with Gunner and his fiancée, through a hazy, dusky midsummer evening at the end of a preposterously hot day. The streets baking with heat. A giant sinkhole had opened in Queens. An unbearable glaze hung over everything. Cars dragging themselves through the glare of Park Avenue. With sunset, a breeze had arrived, fragrant with the smell of hot pavement and something that smelled like cotton candy. We were walking hand in hand, sauntering, and after the dinner—the cute formality of Gunner across from the love of his life—we were relishing a sensation of success. We had raised a gentle soul, a man who tended to his lover's needs and had found someone who would tend to his, and that fact alone seemed sufficient.

Before meeting Gunner and Quinn at the restaurant, Sharon and I had gone to a museum, stood before a Picasso painting of a lobster fighting a cat, and then moved on to examine a Franz Kline, a few wonderful thick blue brush-stokes splayed in crosshatch, and then, downstairs on the cool lower level, a Van Gogh, a small, secret scene of a shadowy figure of a lonely woman, or a man, passing out of (or into) a pedestrian tunnel in the glow of dusk.

As we walked south that evening at a leisurely pace toward Grand Central, we were feeling a contentment that came from the fact that we had passed from the cool, secretive moment together before some of the finest works of civilization, out into the blazing heat, and then into a restaurant on Lexington, and then, two hours later, back out into a cooler dusk alone together.

Years after the fact, I can still feel the vivid sensation of seeing my own situation within the one that Van Gogh had selected for his painting, out of an infinite set of possibilities, and the feeling would linger with me for the rest of my life.

———

That night, somewhere in the Sixties, or perhaps farther south in the Fifties, we glanced to the right and saw what remained of the sunset, framed by the length of the street all the way to the Hudson, a slab of pure lavender light, gloriously perfect, combining with the cold concrete edges.

That's as beautiful as anything Rothko painted, I said to Sharon.

(Oh, dear, wonderful Sharon. Oh, Sharon, love of my life. Oh, beloved sharer of a million eternal moments. Oh, secret lover of secret situations. Oh, you who day by day shared a million intricate conversations.)

That vision has stayed with me. It illustrates how the window looks right now as I sit here with my drink, with the hazy deep blue light edged with the serene, pure black of the window frame, as I sit alone in a room, a year after that night in the hospital, thinking about my wife, about our life together, while the river out beyond the window quivers and shakes with the last sunlight of the day. I have come to believe, in this time of mourning, that only in such moments, purely quiet, subsumed in the cusp of daily life, can one—in the terrible incivility of our times—begin to locate a semblance of complete, honest, pure grace.

In an average life lived by a relatively average soul, what else remains but singular moments of astonishingly framed light?

# LIGHTNING SPEAKS!

D*ear Mom, I'm running away for good. With regrets, your slap-faced daughter*, she wrote in lipstick on the bathroom mirror before heading out the back door, letting it spring behind her in a slam.

She was just shy of sixteen, with hazel-brown eyes and full lips and a tooth gap that Billy found endearing.

Haight-Ashbury boys incarnated across the Great Plains, one shithole town to the next until you got to Michigan, where they staggered, clutched in the palm of the state, operating under the limitations of the peninsula. Freaks who leaned toward bladework, slicing and stabbing. Buck knives in leather holsters, locked in a drifter ethos born in imagined hinterlands.

———

His brand—rubber-stamped on papers, an emblem of his own design: a skull spilling beams of light radiating out to the edges of the sheets; down to the side, his initials: *B. T.*

You're a pill, her mother said. You're a pill. That was the phrase that summer, at the lake. Moving around each other in the cottage; her mother leaning forward into the mirror to apply mascara, putting on her work face, as she called it, though she was out of a job and training to be a medical transcriptionist.

I'm a pill, she told Billy. You certainly are, he said.

*Auris*, ear, her mother said, soaking up to her neck in the claw-foot tub, memorizing the words from her textbook. *Calcaneus*, heel. Heel, like your father, she said, later, moving around the kitchen.

The word *runaway* was a misnomer. She moved in a slow lope, barefoot, down the road that ran behind the small cottages; the water bright blue beyond the weedy yards; the sand nice beneath her feet; the sensation of leaving something behind, certainly, but not in haste. Leisurely, she walked, waiting to hear her mother call.

————

A few years later, on the hospital porch, getting some air, she'd describe it to the patient named Trey, her sidekick during treatment.


Your father's gone, her mother said. Gone. The fucker. All he took were his pipes, his pipe rack, his tobacco, his cufflink box, his bullet box. The rifle, too.


Meg remembered the vinyl tobacco pouch: a plaid pattern with a metal band that opened like a mouth when you squeezed, and then snapped shut over the moist curls.


Her father worked management at Fisher Body and spoke in a distracted, distant voice—except when he razzed her hair, tickled her waist, gave her what he called Indian burns, rubbing his palms into her arm softly and then twisting harder and harder. Friction, he'd shout. Friction makes heat and heat makes pain and pain makes the world go 'round.


Keep digging and you'll go all the way through to China, he said one afternoon from his lawn chair, balancing a tumbler on his knee. The soil was thick and deep, worm-filled, root-tangled. She dug eagerly.

---

Friction, she thought: the murmur of it; her head thrown back while he loomed over her on his elbow; the smell of dead fish—fucking alewives, Meg, Billy said, speaking softly, part inside and part out.

Shaggy willows catching the falling sunlight across the yard, reaching up to sweep their crowns through it as she licked a tab, and, on the bed, he flipped the cash, counting.

Families with wicker baskets and tartan blankets and vacuum flasks used to come here until frightened away by the likes of me, Billy said.

*Meniscus*, her mother said, *medial*, *lateral*, parts of the knee, and that's derived from Greek and was the way they described curved things. You've got my knees, Meg, you're going to have my curves.

Billy liked to throw his head back and roar a laugh that seized and stopped suddenly; he had an alluring jerkiness to his movements: quick lurches, abrupt readjustments of his mouth; she remembers not so much the details as the general physics, seen from her fifteen-year-old self, how he shifted the record over the spindle before letting it drop.

————

I'm so sorry, her mother said, her voice uncharacteristically light, airy, with the smell of bourbon as she pressed in close; the fear, too, inside the words, holding Meg at arm's length and examining her before crying, Oh my God, oh my God, where have you been, what's happened to you?

Help me practice, she said, handing over the flash cards: on one side, the word *phalanges*; on the other, *fingers*. A July afternoon at the end of the dock. Detroit was burning.

The inflated price of STP. A posse of law enforcement offi-cers standing mutely while the bonfire of dope—confiscated from a cottage on the far shore of the lake—burned; the value of a lid shifting as it moved from Chicago to Detroit, or via boat from Canada to Port Huron, draft dodgers going up and product coming back.

It feels like you're down in a deep canyon, caught in there with a herd of animals—goats or sheep or cows, whatever—packed so close they can't move, crushing each other, until an electric prod gets them to separate out, until there's fi-nally a single animal—me!—free, galloping along across the prairie, leaving the earth with each bound, the feet coor-dinated like that photo, you know, the one by Muybridge, Trey said on the hospital porch.

---

Nurse Elana had an outdated bouffant hairdo and a hoarse smoker's voice. There was an anti-voice pill meant to ease the voices that came, and another to counteract the bad things the anti-voice pill did, and another to counteract the things that counteracted the counteraction. They hardly understood the medicines' effects, which was clear in the stern ritual that played out—the paper cups like rattlesnake tails, the mouth check, the pat on the head, and how Elana kindly told her to rest, rattling off with the tray.

Malcolm X's mother was a patient here until a few years back, Trey said. Her name was Louise Little. For all I know, she might still be up there, he said, gesturing over at the tower, where the bars on the windows were thicker.

Trey had hung with a crew that operated out of Bad Axe, bikers running dope from Point Edward, and had known—or at least thought he might've known—someone named Al, an uptight guy who rode an absurdly modified Harley with ape-hanger handlebars—some blacksmith made them up there, he said—that shook like hell and jiggled him around until he had electricity running through his blood.

I myself have gone electric, Trey said, meaning he was receiving electroshock treatments. He disappeared for days, and when he reappeared, they fell back into the routine, leaning into the sorrow that bonded them temporarily, gazing out at the hospital grounds, and the road.

Marv—in olive overalls—shoveled mulch from a wheelbarrow, tossing it around the base of one of the large oaks, and a few cars passed unusually slowly, and she imagined herself a passenger going by the hospital, looking back at the big, looming structure, at the medieval water tower, as she had many times as a kid, holding her nose and making the peace sign, which was something her brother had taught her to do, a weird, kid superstition meant to ward off bad spirits, and then she felt destabilized by the recognition that if you stayed on that road for half a mile, heading south, and took a left on West Maple, it would lead to her old house, a colonial along a tree-lined street.

I was just strolling, and I was thinking, I'm not running away, I'm strolling away, she said.

Yeah, Trey said. That's how it goes. You don't *run* away so much as sort of leave on an impulse and keep going at whatever pace happens to suit you at the time.

It was futile to describe a drug trip, or a vision, and all you'd get from trying was a shake of the head and a laugh and an argument from someone who'd had much better trips. Time would teach her that, eventually.

You told me about the first time you saw him, Billy, when you were out in a canoe with your friend Judy, who ran off with Al. You told me you paddled out there and then saw him on the way back. You got closer to shore, and Judy stood up and started dancing—*go-going* was how you described it, like a go-go dancer. You said she fell in the water after you let go of the gunwale—you used that word, *gunwale*—and then you flipped the other way and went under and wanted to stay there. You told me how you felt down there, that you could get away from your mother, and how the water was murky, yellow, warm, and then you came to the surface but stayed out in the lake, floating, playing it cool, while Judy swam in. You described that, too, must've been a week ago. You told me you watched Judy on the shore, flirting with Billy, dancing on her toes, drying in the sun, and you saw her laugh and throw her head way back with her mouth open, you said that, and then she crawled to him—that's how you told it—and he played her a tune on his guitar, and then you told me about how a day later, after that fight with your mom, he told you he thought that you were cool, staying out in the lake like that, not swimming in, and he said you were cool, Meg. You're cool, Meg, you said he said.

———

Who's Muybridge?

I saw action, and they shipped my ass home, Trey said. There one day, and here the next. I didn't go in for that kiss-the-ground shit, bowing to the tarmac. Folks at the VA in Detroit spelled it out in plain terms. We're gonna release you into the streets, they said, and so I came here, where there aren't streets, at least not like those.

The bell would call them in, breaking the afternoon apart. Mornings in sessions with a group, or a shrink, lunch together at long tables, the air steamy, and then outside on the porch to get air. Then the bell.

Trey's scar from his wrist to his elbow was slow to heal, something he had done, he said, to prove he could still bleed. He'd used the same pruning shears—before he did his arm—to cut his hair, which had grown out uneven. The hospital allowed long hair, offered that one grace to its customers—a ragged bunch of long hair and super Afros and buzz cuts mixed together, all damaged by the spirit of the times.

Now's the time to refill his mind with the bits of her story the current took away, she thought, looking out at the grounds, watching as Marv spun his riding mower around and around another oak, churning up a cloud of dust and chaff.

My mom was living in the past, and that wasn't good for me. That summer, it was just the two of us, alone on the lake after my father split, she said, and then she described how her mother used to take down hatboxes from the closet, musty, round boxes with delicate ribbons, blue and yellow, and she'd lift the hats out and set them on the bed and tell a story about each one, going into great detail about the boys she'd loved, still loved, and in particular a boy named Ted Knapp, who was the love of her life and biggest regret. Ted Knapp this, Ted Knapp that. Ted had the cutest little roadster. Ted came home from the war with a Purple Heart. Ted was an expert kisser. Ted went off to Yale. Ted came home to his father's bank. Ted was killed in the war. Ted survived the war. Ted's family had class. Ted had a nifty little boat.

If you talk to the lightning, you're praying. If the lightning talks to you, you have schizophrenia. One of her doctors told her that.

She talked about how her mother had fought weight gain by eating these waxy cubes of chocolate wrapped in paper that were really just candy but were meant to suppress hunger somehow, and how her mother had treated her like a little girl, calling her a pill, and that had led to a huge fight sometime in July, and how she'd scrawled lipstick on the bathroom mirror, and once the words were on the mirror, she felt an obligation to make good on them, so she walked around the lake to the house where Billy was squatting, feeling the sand and a wonderful sense of not running, of taking her time.

How the tunnel passed under the road—concrete and musty, with the thump of cars overhead, and sunlight seeping between the two lakes, West and Austin, like honey beneath the hull—and then, in the cove on the other side, she and Judy would pull in to shore and smear their legs with mud, letting it dry in the sun, giving themselves an excuse to jump into the cool water to wash it off.

The frontier's closed, Meg, Billy said. You see, in the olden times a young soul could journey into the vast unknown like Odysseus on his ship, and that was his bag, that's my bag, but the thing is, the thing is, every single bit of that world has been picked over, Meg. For us—he was fingering a tab of acid, holding it up—we have to go inward to see new worlds, to make discoveries, and that's what we're gonna do tonight.

Muybridge was this dude who figured a way to photograph moving objects, to stop time, so that you could see the weird, fucking amazing intricacy behind things you took for granted—you know, horses at a full gallop, people doing the foxtrot, that kind of thing, Trey said, lifting his heels up from the porch railing and setting them down gently.

Two patients had each other in a headlock. A clockwork scene. Each afternoon, at least two of them ended in a heap on the gray floorboards. A thump of boots, shouts, the orderlies calling for restraints.

Billy was one of those boys you'd see at a concert clambering up the towers, or the speakers, or at a parade, shimmying up a light pole for a better view, she said.

Yeah, yeah, I get it, Trey said. The type who'll do anything to get a vantage. They'll stomp for what they want. He was rolling a cigarette—his hands steady, working diligently, holding the paper to the blue bag, sprinkling, rolling tight, examining, rolling tighter, then licking the glue.

I might've known Billy, because I knew a bunch of Billys in that scene in Bad Axe, half the crew was named Billy: Billy Goat, this big fucker out of Chicago, Big Billy, who claimed he rode with the Angels out in Anaheim, and it was Billy Goat who kicked my ass for no good reason except maybe this, he said, holding out his hands. My color, I mean.

———

Lightning appeared down the thick, braided wire, a bright-blue glow, dripping and recollecting itself, forming a ball and squeezing through the screen, like cheese through a grater, emerging as a quivering, hovering glob, and then, after emitting a low hum, a little jangled tune, it began to speak in an English accent—kind of like Mick Jagger's, she'd tell Trey one afternoon; and then, for a few minutes, in the afternoon silence, with only the wind in the trees, the shush of it, and the cars on the street, and other sounds, too, the soft roll of the rocker rails on the battered porch and the throb and buzz of cries from inside, through the window bars, she heard the lightning speak, as it had spoken before, and it said:

*There were these two souls, one was older, and he walked with a strut across our land, putting his boot heels forward, his hands strong, squeezing the handlebars of his chopper, as cool as could be. He was from the sky, from the dust, from the lonely afternoons. And there was a girl, young, and there was a shadow between the girl and her mother. The girl had a spark in her heart, a little flame, and she could hear voices inside the long afternoon silence as she rocked on the porch, killing time. The mother didn't know it, but she'd pushed the girl away. That slap on her face would last for eternity, the fingers on her flesh and the pain. Her body was not her own, she had to leave, and then her soul joined the boy's. Together, they saw me and made me, and I was there for them, man, because they made me.*

———

The lightning hissed and sighed.

*I am a violation of natural law. Inside me is the other world, the inverse world, and I'm just a small invasion. You will carry me, Meg, and I will fuel you.*

That afternoon, Trey had her hand in his, squeezing it tight as he spoke, saying, Look, Meg, I don't want to ruin your story or anything. I mean, it's a great one, and I've enjoyed hearing it again. But you should know that whatever significance that vision holds for you comes from the fact that your mind created it.

After it was gone, a hole remained—in the air, above the bed—a membrane that quivered and then, in turn, disappeared, leaving them alone together.

No, he said something like that later, in the hours before she was released, walking to the car, waving to him, watching as he lifted his hand and waved back—that it was the last time she'd see him. It was unfair, but that's the way it was in those days—Trey with his skin a brown like varnished maple. One coat, he'd said, that's all I got was one coat, holding out his arms and smiling in the afternoon light.

———

The nurse who rang the bell that called them in for rest time obviously took great pleasure in the gesture, because there was a long pause between each clang as her arm made a wide arc, and in that pause—with the vibration still resonating out into the green of the grass and the concrete pathways—there was enough quiet to let in the sound of the wind in the trees, and, as they crossed the old, warped porch, Meg was momentarily released from the story and was simply aware of Trey's fingers in her own, twisting gently, quivering with his nervous energy, and when she looked at him, he lifted the corner of his lip to warn her of his coming smile, and there was something in his eyes that told her he regretted what he'd said while, at the same time, he knew he had to say it. And that's exactly what he said as he shrugged his shoulders and, one finger at a time, let go of her, gesturing for her to step ahead of him inside.

The way her father had mixed cocktails, moving his hands and rocking the shaker, holding the strainer with his fingers spread and his eyes on the television screen, filling the glass, lifting the shaker high, letting it sluice expertly. That was how it had felt with Billy those first days, before she understood what she now understands.

Cars on the street seemed to pass with a sort of solemnity, an air that told her they were aware of their freedom in relation to those who watched from the hospital porch, inspecting that freedom.

--------

Judy was called a runaway when she took off with Al, and then, after two months, she became a missing person, and then, after two years, she was presumed dead and gone, or in Canada, or with some commune or something.

Trey arrived rubbing his jaw, pale pink marks above and below his lips where the rubber bit had pressed, and small round spots where the electrodes had zapped his temples. His eyes looked dazed and waxy, bloodshot, inward-drawn, as he sat quietly in the chair, staring beyond the road to a point on the horizon where his memories—the ones lost to the current—were, as he said, stacked like a cord of wood.

I'm into ball lightning. I'm into this shit that happens and then no one believes it, but everyone knows it has to exist because everyone has some kind of ball-lightning story, even if they haven't witnessed it. Am I right? Damn right I'm right, Billy said, and then he went on to tell the story of the time his parents had taken him to a party on Lake Michigan, at a big house near Harbor Springs, and they were out front, watching the storm coming in, laughing at a man who had been sent to make sure the boat was tied to the dock, something like that, and when he was down by the water a bolt came and struck him in the head and he stood there burning.

———

Is it *ball* lightning or *balled* lightning? Judy asked, passing the smoke back to Meg. I say *ball* and he says *balled*, Meg said, and they both laughed.

I argued with Judy that ball lightning was a shared vision, she said. According to Billy, it was a rare thing, that kind of vision. And Judy gave me this look and said the word *cool* in a certain way, flat, toneless, and it was the last thing I remember her saying before she took off with Al.

That was the other side of the universe coming into this one and exposing itself to us, Billy said as the storm rumbled eastward. Above the bed, in the air where the ball lightning had been, an oval membrane quivered, small blue veins beneath the surface as delicate as the skin of a baby's palm. He leaned forward, poked it with his cigarette, and spoke into it, saying, Okay, for what it's worth, paranoia runs deep, man, and that's Buffalo speaking through me, Meg, and anyway this isn't about paranoia, us both seeing the same vision, making it real, he said, now poking his finger through it.

For us, we have to go—he fingered a tab of acid—inward to see new worlds and make discoveries, and that's what we're doing here, together, he said. Then he began talking about how important it was to make sure you charted a course through the center of the whirl. That's it, Meg. The whirl is like a curling wave or a tube, and it goes on to infinity, so you have to stay in the dead center, right there, right here, he said, reaching over to brush the hair away from her face.

A flash, and instant thunder, and the hairs on her thighs stood up, and the wire along the side of the window began to glow, dripping down, seeming to catch and congeal, forming— slowly and quickly—an inverted icicle of current that pulsed and gave off a musical tone and then spun into fibers, gathering and tightening into a ball, textured with little strings, like a ball of yarn, a quivering blue, and then, with a slight up-and-down motion and a hissing sound, the ball pressed through the screen, breaking up into smaller strings and reforming on the other side, hovering and swaying as it passed over their bellies, touching them both as they watched it from inside their highs, aware of their own awareness in a weird way, before lifting up into the middle of the room. That was the second time, she'd explain to Trey.

It was amazing, like a ball of yarn, and it was a shared vision, something like that, and Billy says those are rare, she said to Judy a few days later, when Billy was on a run to Bad Axe. They were in the canoe again, letting the paddles drag as they drifted, looking at his cottage, deep in the shadow of the trees, nothing moving, the porch screens staring back at them while they passed a joint to each other, Judy straightening up to receive it and then lying back to toke, letting the sun, which was coming straight down on the lake, rest on her belly.

Let me show you where it happened, Meg said eventually, because a speedboat had appeared on the water outside, and it had seemed like a bad omen, or it would, later, when Meg recalled the feeling of Judy's hand touching her hand, their legs pressed together on the old couch, passing one of Billy's high-grade doobies back and forth after they'd poked around, opening the fridge in the kitchen, examining the weird oil furnace with a chimney that went into the wall, and then Judy dragged Meg back to Billy's bedroom, laughing as they examined all his bongs and pipes, lined up neatly like surgical instruments on a clean white doily on a table beneath several STP stickers that had been arranged to form an *STP*, and then, leaning on the bed together, stretching out, they stared at the braided wire, hooked to the frame of the window as it came down from the roof. I think you two were just high, Judy said, turning around and looking at Meg. We both saw it, and we both saw the same thing, and he said it was this kind of shared-vision thing. But it was also real, and it connected us in a cosmic way. It came into the room and floated around, and—like I said—it touched us both, and that's the part that Billy told me really means something, Meg said. Cool, Judy said.

The ball lightning was pure prophecy, a sign of their mutual love, bonding them, tripping in union. When she started to speak, Billy raised his hand in the darkness in a way that told her to stop, that nothing she could say would be nearly as important as what he was preparing to say next, a gesture that would become reconfigured just as the ball lightning had become—at least later, in memory—Judy's soul calling out for help.

After a kiss, he pushed her away and held her face in his hands and studied it, making a little *uh-huh* sound, and then his eyes crinkled around the edges, conspiring.

Billy was pacing back and forth on the mossy bank, saying they had to roll at dawn, and then whatever he'd said was lost in the image of his boot, as she clung to the back of the bike, holding on unsteadily, watching as he drove his heel down, again and again, trying to kick-start the engine, until there was a roar and a plume of blue smoke clouding the yard, and then they were leaving, leaving her mother behind, back in the cottage, one of her father's old records playing, something called *Winchester Cathedral*, with a man who seemed to be shouting through an old-fashioned megaphone.

Trey was speaking about the way an idea could leap from one person to the next until no one knew what was really true, or untrue, a mind getting clearer by the minute, along with everyone else's.

———

Don't let that old bag of a mom get you down. Marriage is a mirage, Billy said. That's why the words are so close, Meg, because all you're doing is making a commitment to a dead idea, and then, after a while, the dead idea is all you've got, and the rest—if there ever was anything else—is gone.

She liked Trey's habit of lifting one side of his lip before he smiled, so she knew it was coming, a kind of forewarning of the intensity that seemed to prevail against the pain he suffered.

In bed during rest time, with the drugs sloshing in her belly, she would again feel fully aware of her own awareness, at least it would seem that way, and aware that she'd been high when she saw the ball lightning—inside the same duplicity, two realities.

Some days Trey moved in a jaunty, cute way but didn't say much, and other days he looked sluggish but spoke clearly and urgently again, repeating the description of the deep canyon, the towering stone walls, the animals packed in a herd—goats, sheep, horses, cows, it doesn't matter, Meg, go ahead and take your pick— flank to flank until the electric prod and the separation and then the galloping across—a prairie, or a desert, or a savanna, take your pick—until he was alone, singular—that's the word, Meg, *singular*—with his fucking incredibly coordinated legs.

He said you were cool, Meg. You're cool, Meg, you said he said.

Yeah, that's right, Meg said. Being told I was cool was cool to me when I was fifteen. He said I was cool, and I felt cool.

Yeah, cat rides up and says, Hey, you cool? And you say, Yeah, cool. And he says, Cool, man. Then you feel cool.

One afternoon, on the road, there was what seemed to be a funeral procession, cars moving solemnly with little flags on their antennas, and suddenly Trey stood, throwing his hand to his forehead with a slap, saying, Hot damn, that's got to be military because the lead car is a government sedan for sure, and then he flopped back into his chair and began to cry. Motherfuckers, he said under his breath.

The bell was ringing, the clapper striking the old metal, creating a sound that allowed each one of them to feel her urgency, and everyone was standing except her and Trey because he had his hand in her hand and was holding it tight as he spoke, saying, Look, Meg, I don't want to ruin your story or anything. I mean, it's a great one, and I've enjoyed hearing it again. But you should know that story—aside from what the lightning said to you, which, like I said, I think is meaningful—was all over the state that year. Half the people I knew were tripping and seeing ball lightning, he said.

Marv was out on his riding mower again, cutting a swath through the fallen leaves, sucking them into a bag. A breeze was gusting from the north.

There was a long pause between each clang as the nurse's arm made a wide arc with the old school bell, and in that pause—with the vibration still resonating, swaying out into the green of the grass and the concrete pathways—there was enough quiet to let in the sound of the wind in the trees, and, as they crossed the old, warped porch, Meg was momentarily released from the story and was simply aware of Trey's fingers in her own, twisting gently, quivering—it seemed—with the last faint jolts of electrical current, and when she looked at him, he lifted his lip, and there was something in his eyes that told her he regretted what he'd said while, at the same time, he knew he had to say it. And that's exactly what he said as he shrugged his shoulders and, one finger at a time, let go.

# THE RED DOT

That night at the window, looking out at the street full of snow, big flakes falling through the streetlight, I listened to what Anna was saying. She was speaking of a man named Karl. We both knew him as a casual acquaintance—thin and lanky like Ichabod Crane, with long hair—operating a restaurant down in the village whimsically called the Gist Mill, with wood paneling, a large painting of an old gristmill on a river on one wall, tin ceilings, and a row of teller cages from its previous life as a bank. Karl used to run along the river, starting at his apartment in town and turning back about two miles down the path. He had been going through the divorce—this was a couple of years ago, of course, Anna said—and was trying to run through his pain. As you probably know, rumor has it that his wife had left him for a product designer, a guy who designed toothpaste tubes, product containers. Anna paused, as if to let that rumor rest between us, and I saw in my mind's eye one of the newer toothpaste tube designs, shorter and stubbier than the long tubes of my youth. It seemed important that Karl's wife had run off with a man who designed everyday products, whereas her husband had spent his evenings behind the bar, or at the maître d' station, moving from guest to guest, touching shoulders (he was big on that) as he leaned down to chat, smiling and keeping his diners happy, running back to the kitchen to check on the cook, and, in the late evening, when everyone was gone, staying to close up, making sure everything was tidy, clean. Then sometimes— I knew because, coming home late at night, driving through our dark town, I would see him there—he would sit alone at his restaurant bar, nursing a drink with all of the lights off except the dim ones he left on until dawn. So, Anna was saying, he was going through that horrible divorce, battling in the courts over custody of Ethan and all of that, and he was running along the path in the park late in the morning and stopped at the end to catch his breath, and he sat down. (At the window, we both imagined—I imagine—the spot in the woods with the old stone structure that had served as a bathhouse years ago when folks came up from the city to enjoy a day in the country. You looked at the remains of that stone building, just an outline of the foundation, and felt the intense geographical and psychological shifts that had taken place when the automobile and parkways made a trip up the river feel too close, not far enough from the city.) Anyway, Karl sat down and began meditating, following his breath as it moved in and out of his body, clearing his mind, brushing his thoughts gently away, Anna said—pausing to gaze out the window—and then when he opened his eyes

everything was clear. He said that to me, Anna said. We
bumped into each other at Coffee Klatch last fall, and he sat
down and began spilling his guts. I hardly knew him, but he
told me about how he loves that sensation of opening his
eyes after meditating, when everything is suddenly in focus,
sharp and new. In this case, the river and the leaves on the
trees and, across the river, Croton. When he opened his eyes
he saw, through a break in the trees, something red out in
the water. A red dot, he said, she said. He stood up—I'm
imagining this part, Anna admitted—and watched the red
dot until it grew—he said *materialized*—into the shape of a
red kayak moving toward him from the middle of the river.
Something about the way it moved—it was still too far out
to see clearly—or its speed, something captured and kept
his attention, or perhaps he was still in a meditative state and
simply felt compelled to make the kayak part of his process.
Anyway, what's important is that he kept an eye on it as it
slowly closed in on the shore, coming closer, and then he
decided to walk down to the shoreline—the tide was out,
I assume, Anna added—and he got down to the sand and
watched as it got closer and closer.

Now do you want to hear the weird part? she said. (We
were still at the window, looking out, watching a car move
slowly down the street, pushing through the snow and slush.
She had moved closer to me. I looked into her deep brown
eyes and watched as she hooked a strand of hair behind her
ears. Yes, give me the weird part, I said.) Okay, at this point,
before going on with his story, Karl interrupted himself and
made a huge deal out of telling me that his wife was hor-

rifically afraid of water, didn't know how to swim, and was even afraid to go aboard boats and had refused, one summer, to get on the ferry to Martha's Vineyard. He told me a story about how she had to be sedated, taken on deck in a wheelchair, and kept asleep until just before they were docking in Oak Bluffs. (Can you imagine that? she said, and I said, Yes, I can imagine it.)

So you can probably guess what's coming, she said, and I said, No, I can't guess, I have no idea, and at that point Anna moved a little closer, sipped her drink, smiled, and said, So when this red dot, this kayak, got close enough, he saw it was being paddled by someone who looked a lot like Debbie, his ex-wife. At first he thought: Wow, that kind of looks like Debbie. But when she got even closer, he saw that it was Debbie, and seeing this freaked him out and he ran up the path and into the trees. He told me he went into the trees. There she was, his wife, who was scared of water, in a kayak.

We stood quietly for a moment sipping our drinks and staring out the window at the snow, the black trees scratching the snow-clouded sky. I'm sure we were both imagining Karl's ex, Debbie, and her straight blond hair, and her eyes—set unusually wide in her face—a washed-out blue with threads of white like an old pair of jeans. Then Anna went on with the story: Karl stayed back in the trees and watched as she came ashore, unstrapping herself, getting out, putting her legs in the water, pulling the boat onto the sand, standing next to it for a minute, looking up into the trees and then turning back to the water, crouching down, spreading her feet out a bit (Karl said that), putting her hands on her knees, closing her eyes, and going into what seemed to be a meditative state for a few minutes, stretching her arms straight out toward the water. In the trees, Karl was totally freaked out, remembering the many times she had refused to walk along the shore, to get close to where the waves were breaking, and a particular time when Ethan, at Coast Guard Beach on Cape Cod, waded too far out, his little legs swept out from under him, and, frozen in fear, unable to go into the water, she had screamed for a lifeguard to come to assist her. They had talked often about this fear of water, Karl explained, and had traced it to an origination point, I guess you'd call it, Anna said, all the way to her days as a little kid in Madison, Wisconsin, sailing with her parents on Lake Mendota, zeroing in on one particular afternoon when a sudden gale came out of the blue and her father didn't ease the sail, or whatever you fucking call it (Karl said, she said), and the boat went over; or maybe the fact that her sister had nearly drowned in a similar incident, years later, sailing in a race off the Yucatán Peninsula. He recalled how for a few months after Ethan was born she refused to bathe, or shower, and her fear of water seemed to be—and he admitted that it was just a theory she got from a therapist—amplified as part of her postpartum depression, a desire to dry herself up after all that womb moistness (he used that exact, weird phrase, Anna said, using her palm to wipe a bit of frost off the window). Oh, and her water had broken when she was in the supermarket.

(He told me that, Anna said.) She was at the Stop & Shop, at the cashier, when it broke. Anyway, he stood in the trees and watched while she finished meditating, if that's what she was doing, got up and stretched, working her neck from side to side and then, holding the hull of the kayak, wading into the water and splashing her legs to get the sand off, and then, carefully, using the paddle to establish balance, she got back in the kayak and began to paddle out again. At that point Karl panicked and shouted to her from the trees, saying Hey, or Hey you, or something, and she paddled around and began to start back to the shore, and when she got close enough he walked down the path to the waterline and they had a brutal argument that went on for fifteen minutes (he said that, fifteen), shouting at each other and weeping. He wouldn't tell me what they fought about, said they were both crying, but he admitted that he did say, near the end of the argument: Who the fuck are you? What the fuck are you doing out on the river? And Debbie said, I'm enjoying a water sport, that's what I'm fucking doing, and then she turned and began paddling furiously, and he watched until she was a red dot again, far out in the middle of the river, and then he sat on the shore and continued watching as the current drove the dot north, out of sight where the river turns. (We continued to look out the window. There were a few guests behind me—I'd used a similar scene, I thought, in a short story—the shush-shush of the cocktail shaker, the sound of Andy the filmmaker talking about his documentary about Neil Young. Neil let him hold his guitar, Old Blue, or Old Roy, whatever he calls the thing, he was saying, his voice booming over the din.)

———

Weird, I said. That's a weird story. So first he told you about her fear of water, and then he continued the story and told you about seeing her from the shore? Well, actually, I'm gonna have to explain something, she said, lifting her glass to her lips, tapping it to get an ice cube to slide into her beautiful mouth. You haven't heard the twist yet. I have to give you the punch line.

Give me the twist.

Here's the twist. When the kids were little and I was on leave from the firm, I was going insane with boredom, so I started swimming at the Y in the afternoons, doing laps, and there was a woman who always swam with me, usually in the next lane, and she was this amazing swimmer, I mean she would lap me again and again, working those amazing shoulders that were like a yoke, just huge, and one afternoon after I finished I took a shower and then got in the sauna. I was in there for a few minutes and then she came and joined me and we sat and didn't say anything for a while and then she turned and we started talking and she told me she was married to the guy who runs the Gist Mill, and I said, Hey, yeah, Karl, and she said, Yeah, and we talked a bit and I got around to joking about how she laps me and she explained that years ago at the University of California she made the Olympic team, was on the secondary squad, or whatever they call it, and from that point on, when we swam together, we ended up in the sauna talking. Anyway, we became close, you know, in the way you do with someone in the sauna after working out, talking about kids, about ADD, about the school board, the PTA, and the town planning stuff, and I remember we talked about the Ferber method—she was trying to get Ethan to start sleeping on his own, I remember that, Anna said. She was letting him cry, counting the minutes. Then you'd increase the minutes and the crying would keep going. She told me Karl freaked out, tore a few pages out of the Ferber book. The kid cried for two hours and they huddled out in the hall, barely able to stand it, but eventually the kid fell asleep on his own but then started this weird thing of not wanting them around at all at bedtime, no tucking in or any of that. But before Ferberizing the kid—that's what she called it, saying, We had to Ferberize the kid—before that he was coming into bed with them and they were going crazy, and here's the thing that I remembered after Karl told me his story. I remembered that she had mentioned once, in the sauna, that she liked to kayak in the mornings. She got up at the crack of dawn and kayaked along the shore while Karl and the baby were asleep. I remember because she told me that once the kid had been Ferberized she had a chance to sneak out and kayak. She used that word, *sneak*. I remember that.

As we stood at the window, someone was laughing loudly behind us, deep snorts and guffaws, and someone else turned the music up, Bob Dylan snarling and choking his way through "Here Comes Santa Claus."

Okay, so why didn't you interrupt him in the Coffee Klatch and say something like, Hey, I thought Debbie loved to swim, something like that? I said, and she said, I don't know, perhaps it says something about my personality that I didn't interrupt him, that I was so intrigued—I mean he was practically sobbing into his coffee—that he seemed to be making shit up, or perhaps he really thought she was afraid of water. Perhaps she hid her love of swimming and water from him.

She paused and we both nodded, looking out at the snow, and said, Yeah, yeah, at this idea. Maybe she snuck off to the pool while he slept late in the morning, or past noon into early afternoon, and faked a fear of water at the beach to get out of the fucking tedium of taking care of the kid, or maybe it began as her way of not dealing with those horrible few months after the baby was born, the jet-lag exhaustion, the nails-on-a-chalkboard of the crying baby, maybe this fear was originally fake and then overcame her and became real, something like that.

We turned around and, still talking, went to the kitchen to get another drink, and then we went back to the window. Perhaps Karl just had to bullshit his way through his pain, one of us said, and then, in a joking manner, we agreed that the version I'd come up with was the best: this fear of water was something she had conjured up to manipulate Karl, some manifestation of a deeper problem in their marriage, arriving out of the long afternoons of tedium and the loss of your sense of self that comes from being with a child all day—and now I see how strange it was that we both agreed that this perverse version was the one we liked the best: betrayal and deception on the part of Debbie instead of Karl being in a weird place, mourning his loss, making up bullshit to explain himself. Now, to be honest, I think maybe Debbie really did fake a fear of water and Karl, from his point of view, was being truthful about everything he said in the story he told Anna at the coffee shop, and I even think, now, after all this time has passed, that somehow both of us at the window that night were foreseeing—or having a prophetic vision, or something like that—that Karl would, as soon as spring arrived and the ice along the shore melted, attempt to swim across the river to Croton, digging in with his stroke as the current in the middle of the river drew him north until, presumably, he ran out of steam, or got hypothermia, and let go—and he was taken, or rather his body rode the tide, all the way past Bear Mountain, to Cold Spring.

I still think about that story. Not the beginning or the end, not the sense that I had—the perplexity—when I held the entire thing, but that time at the window just before Anna filled me in on the second part, told me the twist about the swimming and the Y and all of that. She had restrained herself from telling me that part up front. She could have told me her side of the story first, giving me the pool and the swimming and then the sauna and then getting to Karl's story at Coffee Klatch second, putting an emphasis on how strange he was that day in the coffee shop, and her inability to inter-rupt him, to say, Hey, wait, I thought Debbie loved the water. Looking back now I remember more than anything the feel-ing I had as we stood at the window that there was some elegiac beauty in the scene, however delusional it might have been, of visionary Karl as he finished meditating and opened his eyes to the bright reality of the world he was in—no matter how horrible he felt, after the court battles, the alimony, the fight over Ethan and the house and his restaurant—to spot the red dot. Why can't we simply honor his befuddled, mind-blown bewilderment? The strange way the world can turn inside out? The majesty of his wife's phobia!

Stop. Leave it right there, I wish I'd said to Anna. Leave it pure mystery. I wish I'd turned from her and walked back to the kitchen to get another drink, where maybe I would've been drawn into a conversation with someone else, letting the part about the pool and swimming remain unspoken. I wish my wife, Sharon, had come up to me right then— she was sitting with her drink, chatting up Bruce, ignoring me because we had fought on the way to the party about a late car payment, and I know if she'd come in to refresh my drink she might've caught me at the window with Anna, detected some illicit conspiratorial erotic energy in our postures. Better yet, I wish Karl had been at that party that night so I could've buttonholed him into a long conversation about something, music, anything, and maybe somehow, just by hanging out with him and talking about his failed marriage, changed some small aspect of his life, something tiny but enough to butterfly-effect his fate in some other direction, just as I often wish that I had gone— when I was younger, when I had the opportunity—to the funeral of my good friend's father in St. Louis, where I would've also been with the writer, my friend's other best friend, and if I'd gone, and I know this is a preposterous, egotistical thing to imagine, but I still do it, maybe we would've bonded and become close friends and maybe, just maybe, I would've done something to change his own fate.

The town showed up en masse for Karl's memorial. It wasn't a head-shaker, the fact that he'd tried to swim across the river. He'd talked about swimming the river—people confirmed that when they got up to ruminate. His chef, a young man with a goatee, said Karl was a good swimmer and a hard-core runner. A few years ago he had participated in a river challenge for charity, making the swim from Beacon to Newburgh, a narrower part of the river, to raise money for heart disease, so it wasn't such a shock that he gave it a shot on his own, his prep cook explained. His business partner, Bruce, spoke of his love of the restaurant, his kindness, his ability to balance his duties of serving his guests with running an efficient operation, and then, lowering his voice, he spoke of Karl's love of the Hudson River, his support of Riverkeeper, an organization dedicated to cleaning up the water. Then someone named Anna Carthright, extremely old, unfolding her body into a standing position, her fist around the end of a cane, wobbled her way slowly to the microphone and, leaning down, in a husky, smoky voice—startlingly strong—told a story about him as a teenager growing up in Yonkers above his father's shoe repair shop, and the way he liked to stand with his father at the tooling bench, watching him at work, and, yes, he had been a fantastic high school swimmer, winning the state championship three years in a row. Then she began to weep in that sour way of the aged—consumed, it seemed, with a glut of old memories.

Many got up and spoke, each one taking a turn at filling in the pieces, talking about his wit—who else would come up with the Gist Mill as a name? The Gist Mill, "where you go to get the gist of good food," one of the early ads in the local paper exclaimed. At the end, walking quickly to the front, Debbie, in a short black dress with straps over her shoulders—yes, wide, really wide, swimmer's shoulders—and her hair, brilliantly blond, brittle from the chlorine, got up to read from a poem Karl had loved by Wallace Stevens, about a blue guitar, and then Ned Patterson came to the front of the church and played his trombone, an original piece he'd written in honor of Karl, based on another Stevens poem about a jug, or a jar, or something in the hills of Kentucky, or perhaps it was Tennessee, and when he was finished—not a dry eye in the house, as they say—everyone went out of the church and stood in the blinding sun, blinking and shaking heads as if amazed that the clear, beautiful day existed, the way I imagined Karl had shaken his head and blinked in disbelief after he meditated in the woods that day, catching sight of that red dot in the water, watching as it materialized into his wife.

That afternoon we gathered at the funeral parlor for the viewing, signing the book, pretending to gaze down at his body, avoiding it, really, many of us just glancing—the long face, the powdery cheeks, the purplish lips—and then some of us headed outside to smoke, to talk about his restaurant, his ability to make us feel at home, the cozy nature of the Gist on a snowy winter night, his ability to hire and hold on to great bartenders, his subtle wit, how much he meant to the town, this and that, smoking second cigarettes, glancing back at the door, avoiding going back in because it would mean navigating the various clusters of family members, older friends from college. We stayed out as long as we could, watching a few latecomers come up the walk and enter while a few others came out, walked in the opposite direction, drove away. Gradually the conversation moved to the other big topic at hand: the death of our town's most famous and beloved figure, the film director—who had been a good friend of Karl's and even put him in a bit part in one of his films, the one that won an Academy Award—and how the director had somehow avoided being a snob, kept a casual involvement with the town while still maintaining a gravity field (someone said) around him, and then someone laughed and said: Hell yeah, he had a fucking gravity field, no fucking doubt—and financed local art shows and as an anonymous but obvious donor built the new wing on the library. Somehow that got us talking about the second-most-famous town member, who owned a house on the river and drummed, was the drummer for the biggest band in the world, or at least the band that claimed it was the biggest in the world and probably was, although the guys in the band were a bit old, threadbare, retreading (someone said) their old sounds, having a so-called comeback every few years. I stood there smoking my third cigarette and resisted telling the story of how I had met the drummer one afternoon, walking the dog on Broadway, noticing him as he came in my direction holding his little boy's hand, and they stopped to pet the dog and I said hello and told him I particularly liked his work on that side project, the country singer's album, a comment I'd had at the ready for such a chance encounter, and instead of being pleased to hear it, to know that I actually recognized his accomplishments outside his super huge band, he gave me a gruff reply, with an Irish lilt, the words indiscernible, really, and without saying another word, with his kid in tow, he walked away, making me consider, for the rest of that afternoon, the nature of that kind of fame, how it formed a shield around you, nobody really responding to you as a human but rather to something else, something that formed around their sense of you, something like that, or maybe the other way around, who knows, and when I was thinking about that—on the porch of the funeral home, smoking that third cigarette— I thought about Karl, how he had taken a firm, human form as one of our local notables, kind and witty without being too close, sort of a middle ground, known and yet still somehow unknown, and how that made the mystery of his story, and his wife's story, and the fear of water or no fear of water, all the more believable because it could be slotted right into the somewhat fuzzy nature of his identity as it presented itself to the town, or to me at least, and how the famous drummer, known for being the one guy in the band who didn't take any shit, didn't really like the fame game, was always in the shadow of the lead singer, who was a blowhard but still seemed like a man who cared about the world, was unable to be like Karl, could not find the middle ground between complete anonymity and stardom in our little town, something like that. And I thought about how he had looked at me that day, his face much older than I'd

expected, just before he turned without saying so long, or
goodbye, or have a nice day, and walked back through the
electric gate at his house, which opened with a very faint
buzzing sound and then, still buzzing, slid shut while my
dog, who had started barking when he turned and began
walking away, barked and barked and barked at the drummer and his little boy and then, after they had disappeared,
continued barking at the gate itself, as if it were alive, and I
supposed it was alive in his eyes, having moved of its own
accord, and then I stood holding the leash and let him bark
a while longer—he had an extremely loud bark for such a
little dog—as I continued thinking about the nature of
fame, how you must feel the sense that people have built
the story around you before they really know you, making
them untrustworthy, perhaps, a normal feeling for anyone
in a small town but amplified somehow, so that the entire
world, from China to Brazil to Poland to Spain, would seem
like a small town to you, everyone knowing your face and
name, or at least, in his case, the die-hard fans knowing it—
whereas for the lead singer everyone in the fucking world
knew him, almost everyone, and his nickname *was* his name
now. And on the porch I thought how with Anna's help I
had projected onto Karl various stories, knowing only a
little bit of hearsay about his life, I thought, watching another pair of mourners leave, a short man with a hat on, a
real hat, a derby, and bowed legs, and his wife, stout—maybe
the correct term is now *large-boned*—walking about a yard
behind him, and then my wife came out and silently told
me, with her glance, that I had failed in my duties by coming out with the smokers, and by smoking myself, and I

gave her a glance that, I hoped, said, Thank you for doing it for me, because I could assume that she had gone the extra mile in politeness with the family members.

Almost a year after the funeral I had a dream that I was eating at the Gist Mill and Karl was there, with a small hand towel over his shoulder, near the back, watching his diners, keeping things going, rushing over to pepper a dish or check in with someone, reaching out, touching shoulders and bowing down and leaning back—his long, lean form elegant, his beard trimmed short and neat—and he came to our table and asked us how things were and we talked briefly about the new bridge that was being constructed across the Tappan Zee, how quickly they were building it, and then we talked about the dredging that had to be done to build the new bridge, and he might've mentioned something about Pete Seeger, or something about the need to clean up a toxic site upriver, or maybe it was something about the tides running high this year, or the ice that had built up during the last deep freeze, and then he went off to tend to his other guests. He was the same Karl, maybe a little bit of grief around the corners of his eyes, something like that, but basically, as far as I could tell when I woke up, the same man, same person. But then a few nights later, I had another dream, one that felt like a sequel to the previous dream. In that dream I was coming home late from the city on a snowy winter night, the streets dead and the town shut down, and I saw him alone at the bar, same towel over his shoulder, holding a glass. I pulled over and parked and tapped on the window with one knuckle, and he looked up and waved me in and I said, Is it too late, you closed? And he said, No, come in, man, let me get you something, and he poured me a huge glass of something golden, some dream drink, and we sat and talked for a while. This time, aware that I was aware that I was in the kind of dream in which you're aware that you're in a dream, I tried to nudge the conversation around to his wife, to the water, to that afternoon along the path in the state park. I asked him how he was doing. I told him what a tragedy it was that he had died. I asked him how it had been out in the water. He told me it wasn't suicide, not exactly, unless you believed that Karl Menninger shit. And yes, he said, I'm named after Karl Menninger, the shrink. Then he told me how he had a wet suit and his tide charts and had it figured for the ebb but then he realized too late, far out in the water, maybe a mile out, with a cold, wintry sky overhead—a front was heading down from Albany but he figured he had it timed right— that he had used last year's tide chart, and when he got out into the middle of the river he could feel the fingers (weird dream language) of current pulling him, a big hand. And right then my dream lost all shape, turned surreal, and he was telling me to calm down because I was in the water, too. But I was much younger in the dream, just a kid in an old orange canvas life jacket, and it was clear that we were both going to drown together because fingers appeared beneath the surface, real dream fingers, and then I saw my teenage car floating past, the old Nova with its sandblasted roof full of hailstone dents, pocked as if from acne, and I realized in that flat-out indescribable dream-logic flash that those were

God's fingers, and we had conspired together in our own delusional self-deception. Oh well, suffice it to say there was a flotation device, the pocked roof of my old car, Karl's face, the river, the current, finger things, the sky, a sense of being in the dream, God's fingers, and Karl next to me with a fiendish grin on his face.

Karl's body had washed ashore in Cold Spring. That wasn't a dream. Sharon and I went up there a few years after some trouble in our marriage to meet with what we referred to as a financial adviser, parking up the road and walking down the hill—some stores open for business, others shut down, boarded up—with the Hudson at the bottom and Storm King Mountain looming beautifully in the dusky summer twilight. We went through the tunnel under the railroad tracks and stood there in the little park, listened to the sound of distant gunfire from the West Point firing range booming off the mountain and back to us, and looked at the river and, right then, I had to resist telling her the story Anna told me that night, because to even mention her name would've been painful, and I'd have to explain right there, with the river flowing swiftly, that I wished she had come to the window that night, interrupted Anna's story, cut us off right then so that I wouldn't know the entire thing but also because then, well, then one thing would not have led to another. I looked at the water and thought: She'd understand, actually, if I told her the entire thing—even the dream, all of it—but then I'd have to be precise and clear about everything and, with the beautiful scene before us, with the warmth that came from the sweet night air, a mix of tidal salt and creosote, it just didn't seem worth it. We were both thinking—I'm sure—about Karl and his restaurant and the tragedy of his swim in the river. We were both thinking, I'm sure, about the dangerous currents that ran all the way up the estuary, dug deep by retreating glaciers, or volcanic activity, a ridge meeting the sea so that the sea and the river battled each other twice a day, if you want to look at it that way, or, better yet, lovingly embraced each other in a mutual, moon-drawn embrace, running silently through the darkness of night and in the heat of day past all the human folly and abject sadness we create when we're here, as it would when we were long gone—just bones and earth—as it had before we were here, I thought. Then I turned and took her hand, or she took mine, I'm not sure now, and we walked under the tracks—the wet dripping of water, the smell dank—and back into town, searching for a cozy little place to eat, anticipating that sensation we'd get, only a few miles away from home, of being on an adventure together in a strange place with strangers all around, and the polite silence of those who do not know who you are.

# I AM ANDREW WYETH!

I f I remember correctly—and I believe I do—I asked Christina to bring the agreement with her to Grand Central Station for an initial meeting about a week before Christmas. Arrive with it signed, if you don't mind, I told her over the phone. We found a table in the food court on the lower level and sat down together, and I explained right away that my reasoning behind having her sign the agreement wasn't so much about my being secretive, or wanting to hide behind a legal document, but really about the document allowing me to maintain—I believe I said—an appearance of intentional isolation. Thanks to the agreement, I could share my thoughts with her without resorting to self-editing—I believe I used that exact term, *self-editing*—and then she smiled slightly as I went on to explain that I wasn't a secretive person. I'm not a soul inclined to withhold, I said. As a matter of fact, I'm the kind of person who feels compelled to make confessions, and perhaps by having you sign this piece of paper I'm building a structure in which my secrets can be kept externally, outside my own mind, so, for example, if I start to tell you about my family, meaning my sisters and my parents, I'll do so knowing that my words, while being heard, will also be reaching a safe, terminal home. Whereas if you refused to sign that agreement, I said, pointing to the contract in her hands, I might feel compelled to begin confessing this and that anyway, partly out of a sense that you're a good listener, and I can tell you are by the way you touch your ear now and then, adjusting your hair away from your cheeks (she had a habit of taking a strand or two of her long auburn hair and tweezing, tweezing, and then carefully, with deliberateness that I found absurdly charming, placing it behind her ear, which was small and delicate). If you don't sign the contract, I'll view you as a conduit to the outside world. Because that's the way I work. I mean I've had a habit in the past of talking to people—usually untrustworthy people—with an awareness that, for example, when I tell them that my father was a bad drunk, and that he fell down the stairs one winter afternoon when I was fifteen and broke three ribs, and that I was the one who dialed for the police, they'll take that information, share it with others, embellishing, bending my words into their own (*His father was a junkie, and fell down the stairs and broke six ribs*), and then pass it on to someone who will do the same until the story I originally told no longer relates to my past but to the past of several imaginary people, floating around out there as a story about *my* father.

I told her this, and, as a way of giving another example, told her about the time my sister stole a check out of a mailbox. I described the mailbox, one of those apartment mailboxes with the little slot for the name and address, with a small, useless cellophane window, and a key that only the mailman was supposed to have, along, perhaps, with the building super, and how he opened up a long row of boxes all at once. I explained how my sister stole the key from the super's office, or perhaps she got there when the mailman arrived and grabbed it when he wasn't looking (I wasn't sure, I added) and then very carefully took the check back to her room at the halfway house and forged a signature. It was a government child-support check for five hundred dollars, and she cashed it at the bank down the street from her halfway house, not far from the Michigan State Capitol building. What's important, I believe I told Christina, is that one wouldn't think my sister would have the skill to pull it off, not only to forge the signature but also to take it to a teller and persuade her, or him, to cash it without the proper identification. Anyway, I believe I said, you see, if we didn't have the nondisclosure agreement I'd tell you this story and then you'd tell someone else, and I trust you'd stick mostly to the facts because you seem like the trustworthy type, but they wouldn't stick to the facts. To add some zest to my original version, they'd say my sister stole a thousand dollars. They'd say she was a kind of idiot savant, brilliant at forgery, able to replicate just about any kind of document, and then someone else, passing it on, would make it a mailbox at the house of some renowned Michigan personage, a state senator, perhaps, and they'd describe how she snuck up to the front door on a clear, cool fall day, or perhaps they'd even make it my hometown instead of Lansing, because they'd know at least that fact about my past, and they'd be telling it with a relish that comes from passing an inside bit of gossip about a reclusive artist, one who has been obsessively painting scenes of the Pennsylvania countryside for the last fifteen years.

In the past—I explained to Christina—my mouth was a conduit for the flow of information outward. In the past I told personal anecdotes that were carefully shaped to allow for the future filling in, or, rather, fictionalization, by souls who didn't know me. I took into account the way a bit of narrative might get passed from a close friend, a kindhearted person with the best intentions, to someone removed from me who would take the story and turn it against me, so that somehow I would be implicated in the story. For example, a mean-hearted person might say that I was the one who taught my sister how to forge a decent check, and how to persuade a teller to cash it. (I did teach her how to forge a check, and I did talk to her about the nature of teller work and how to be usefully confusing in a transaction at the counter, but that's beside the point.)

Then we were on our second coffee and she explained (in a voice that I now see was slightly too firm, too officious, I think) that she would be delighted to be my assistant, and that whatever I said—and she said this, I swear—would stay *in her mind*, and in her mind only, from that moment on, for the rest of time itself (she said that: *the rest of time*), and then she seemed to blush, touched her ear again, and ever so gently lifted her cup and sipped in what seems to me now, looking back, to have been a conspiratorial gesture, as if between us the confidentiality agreement was not only words

on the page but a sacred blood-sealing—ah, I don't know
how to put this!—as if our future together were inexplica-
bly entwined with the fact that whatever I told her about
my work, my plans for a new sequence of paintings, or the
fact that I felt fraudulent on occasion, would stay tucked
away in some corner of her mind forever. Yes, right. I'll die
with your words still in my mind, she said, laughing lightly,
shaking the contract, which rested in her hands, waiting to
be passed over to me.

Like I said, it was a holiday. Grand Central was a bustle of
consumption. A few tables away, in a dark corner, a home-
less man was sleeping with his head on his bag, snoring
softly. Another man—dressed in a ragged army-issue coat—
was resting casually with his hip against a trash can, looking
across the room while his hand, down at his side, groped
steadily for something in the trash. At another table, a woman
in a bright red coat, her face still flushed from the cold, sat
forlornly with a paper cup of soup in her palm, holding it
high as she spooned it into her mouth. The two cops at the
table across from us sat at a slightly odd angle, facing in our
direction, hands flat on the tabletop, sitting straight up in
what seemed to be an obtrusive posture, glancing my way
from time to time with speculative, accusatory eyes, as if
they had built a case against me—based on all of the rumors,
I think I thought—and were waiting to strike when the time
was right. From the hip of the one closest to me the hand-
cuffs dangled, jiggling slightly.

The contract was a single page, copied on both sides—a
standard confidentiality agreement (or nondisclosure agreement) with boilerplate lingo, heretos and therefores in a

stately font—that my dealer had given me to send to her, and it looked, in her fingers, feeble and delicate. Her nails were bright green and her thin fingers had small flecks of paint on one knuckle. When I looked up she looked away from me with an abstracted, vague glance, her lips pressed softly together, puckered, and then she turned and met my gaze as if to say: Look inside my skull, fucker, and you'll see where your words are going to go and you'll see, in the soft gray matter, in that spongy matter, the exact place where I'll keep them (your words) forever, and when I'm dead, rest assured, this gray matter will decay, along with it the things you told me and the things I witnessed as your assistant. (Later, when she was in my studio in Pennsylvania, I would tell her that I felt, at times, like a half-baked Andrew Wyeth, and that at times I felt that my appropriating his life was somewhat dubious. My appropriation of Wyeth was my shtick—I'd say—the entire thing, right down to painstakingly reconstructing his nineteenth-century schoolhouse studio at Chadds Ford on my own plot of land on Long Island, and calling most of my models Olga, and using one of his original, albeit much older now, local models. I swear, and this might seem absurd but it's true, that even there in Grand Central, with two cops seated at the table next to us, I foresaw the fact that I'd use the word *shtick* and then confess that I felt, at times, completely fraudulent.)

At Grand Central that afternoon, sitting down in the food court, just after she touched the contract, just before she picked it up and handed it to me, waving it in the air so that it twisted into the shape of a boat hull, I believe I said to

Christina: I have a feeling that in a few weeks, most likely at my studio in Pennsylvania, which as you know is actually in Long Island, some extremely personal confessions of mine will put me in a bad light—even for you—and if those confessions were to be released into the public mind, or passed on, as I explained, it would hurt my career, not only now—I mean saleswise—but also its critical reception in the future. So I'm saying now, I mean I'm telling you this now as a way to abnegate the mirror—ah, I don't know what I'm saying, I said, and right at that moment, after I spoke and before she spoke, I felt the threshold between us that had been created not only by the contract itself, which was legally binding as soon as she passed it to me, but also by the exchange we had just had and by the milieu itself, the jaunty holiday vibe in the air, and, Jesus, it was in the air, the music was going and commerce apparent in the ceremonial bustle of movement up the escalator over her head, and in and out of doorways to my right as folks poured out of trains and headed to the streets and, some of them, up Fifth Avenue to some event at Rockefeller Center. Gifts were being purchased, wrapped up, tucked into bags, and conveyed to the station while we sat together having our meeting, making a secretive, totally incognito mutual agreement. There wasn't a boundary between us, but rather a threshold just above her mouth, starting at her lips and spreading to her nose and up to her eyes and then out to her ears, which months later, I imagined as I sat there, I might attempt to kiss while she stood listening to me at the window in the studio. A threshold through which my words would pass, entering the confines in which they would rest forever so long as she maintained the terms of the contract, which I gently unfolded and turned over as I examined her signature: the aggressive looping curl of her *C* and the soft snakes of her *s* and the cross of her *i* tapering off to a tiny *a*, as if her strength had given out at the end. In general it was a weak signature. It started strong but flagged in the end.

What else can I do—I believe I thought—but entrust myself to this signature and these clauses and the expression she gives of being willing to hold my words and actions and to retain them, to refuse to release them into the world? And then I said, I think, Look, you'll also have to keep to yourself—I mean as part of this agreement—everything you see, not only in my work space but in the house and out in the field. My process, I mean. You'll have to keep quiet about that, I said, and then I sat there and imagined that we'd go out to the stone wall and follow it slowly for an entire afternoon, quietly (a brisk but relatively bleak autumn afternoon, with a long scrim of clouds smearing the western horizon, at the bottom of the slough), trying to find the exact right subject for my next study. I'd have her put an old whaling oar on the top of the wall. I already knew this, sitting there in Grand Central. I imagined us walking together in that quiet reverie as I pondered the wall and she, in turn, pondered me as I pondered the wall, as I searched for an inspirational quirk in the set of the stones, the handiwork of some lonely man a hundred years ago, some farmer with resolve and grit, a clenched-mouthed man with a furrowed brow and whiskers on his chin and that weather-beaten, New England, wiseacre gravitas. (Like Wyeth, I saw faces in the corn! I saw a toothless man in a stalk without the kernels exposed! I saw a toothy woman in peeled-back folds exposing kernels!)

Christina sat across from me with her face suddenly serene, and a slight down of peach fuzz on her upper cheeks and her earlobes. She had fantastic lobes. They were pendulous and out of proportion to her delicate ears, but not in a way that detracted—somehow, miraculously, I later thought—from the symmetry, which much later would remind me for some reason of the shape of the contract itself just before she handed it over. (If I have one talent, it's an acute memory for shapes, for the strange, intricate spaces between objects. I can still remember a particular set of stones in a wall not far from a small town called Edale, in England's Peak District, where I went in the summer to sketch some studies before I officially began to appropriate Andrew Wyeth. I remember the path and the cattle gate, with the MIND THE GATE sign, and the way the fields spread up into a sharp grade and then, over the hump of the hill, began rolling way down into what might be called a knoll. About fifty yards from the cattle gate was a wall—built with an urgency that was visible in the set of the stones near the ground—with a spot where the mason, or farmer with great skills, had struggled to make use of two rather large stones, hedging them in, tightening them with a few filler stones, forming a gap of about two inches wide, shaped like a turnip. I still remember that turnip. Not the stones themselves, but the turnip. Just as I remember—

now, here alone in my cell, as I like to call it, at the institute, as they like to call it, at the window looking down on the rubber-floored yard with the chain-link fence, where other prisoners, as I like to call them, patients, as they like to call them, smoke and clench the fence, gazing through the trees at the river beyond the roar of the parkway—the exact shape of her lobes in the stale light of the food court.) I imagined in Grand Central that we'd take a direct flight together to Manchester, hire a cab to Edale, and walk that wall at a ridiculously slow pace, and that I'd stop and explain to her that I would know what I was looking for when I saw it, and that I was trying as best I could to get into the obsessive, somewhat reclusive, isolated mind of Wyeth. I'd explain (and I think I did explain) that my goal was to find a state that was even more obsessive and persnickety than Wyeth's. I'd like to go beyond my capacity to be Andrew Wyeth and in pushing beyond his somewhat narrow, obsessive concentration on his subjects—rolling fields and walls and his models, always lonely-looking, slightly abject—I'd surpass him so that if you dialed back in order to account for the fact that I was only appropriating him, I would land squarely on actually being him. I'd explain all of this and then I'd remain silent (and I think I did remain silent) for another hour or so while I waited for the light to shift down into the bottom of the so-called slough. (It wasn't really a slough. A slough is a swamp. But this was the lowland at the dip in the valley where water often collected.) She'd sit on the ground with her legs tucked beneath her—Christina style—and her head back slightly, craning her neck while I made quick, preliminary studies, lifting my hand up after each stroke with a flourish, making sure she saw absolute concentration and commitment to the end of each stroke.

Your duty, I'd explain as we walked along the wall in Edale, is to watch me work and to record it all in your head and to hold it inside forever without revealing it to anyone, as stipulated in the contract you handed me in Grand Central, and in that manner other people—buyers, art collectors—will feel, without knowing why, the implicit secretiveness of my endeavor at some point in the future, years hence, when all that's left of my work is the work itself and a parcel (I would use that word, *parcel*) of biographical information, which will include—because I'm keeping a detailed journal— our meeting in Grand Central and our written agreement, sealed not only in ink but also in my lust and desire, because I'll record that, too, just as I'll record that we worked together for years in a union of mutual silence, a marriage of sorts, and that biography will include the fact that you went to your grave—as you said you would—with my secrets. Far in the future your presence in my working life will add not only an element of glamour—is there anything more glamorous than a confidentiality agreement?—but also a sense, around the vow of silence, that there was something fantastically interesting being kept at bay, forever, for eternity, I explained, as she nodded slowly, in what I mistakenly saw as a conspiratorial way, leaning forward slightly. The two cops were getting up from the table across the way, shifting their guts, moving the leather of their belts around. (Reminding me of the time the cops came to arrest my sister,

arriving at the door with the same leathery shift of guts.)
Down the escalator a woman came with a big red bag resting on the handrail, and then I'm speaking again, or rather
was speaking—and now I'm remembering, of course, not
verbatim but as close as I can get, and I was explaining how
at times, I mean times like this, I believe I qualified, I'm not
sure how much real life can bear art and art real life, because
the two entwine themselves only up to a delicate thin line
(or point) where memory, desire, and touch start to move
away from each other, repelled by the present moment, and
then I reached out and took her hand, held it for a minute,
and then regally kissed the top of each of her knuckles and
then the tip of each of her fingers, while she seemed—it
seems to me now—to hold herself still in a way that reminded me then and, I imagined, would remind me again
and again for some reason, not only of that day in Edale
when we would walk along the wall, but also innumerable
other moments, mainly in my studio back in Chadds Ford,
when I would stand back from a painting and try to get a
perspective—that pale ochre, dusky light coming through
the windows!—while she sat off to the side, quietly (perhaps
even bitterly) observant, holding herself at a remove (she
had that kind of beauty. She struck delicately quiet poses—
with her back straight and her hands at her sides, or on her
knees—that seemed to speak of desolate isolation) in a pose
that would remind me of Emily Dickinson; the same prim-
ness of her visage, a beautiful, resilient tightness in her pose.
As I kissed her fingers—weirdly, awkwardly—she presented
for the first time that pose. Then, as she listened to my apol-
ogy, I explained to her that it wouldn't happen again and

that the agreement she had signed in no way excused me from any kind of abhorrent behavior, which of course she would not have to keep secret. (Abhorrent behavior toward you, I explained. Not toward the work, or toward others, or toward the landscape, so to speak, I believe I said.) I was anticipating moments of rash destruction to come, because even there—amid that holiday cheer, the tight clip of heels against the smooth floors, the wonderfully anachronistic announcements of the train departures, and the police, who were now getting up from the table, still looking our way— I had a sense that the signed and sealed document on the table between us would allow for certain shared secrets that might or might not cause a tear in the fabric of the universe (call it love, call it whatever you want) on some future date, when whatever she saw and heard was eaten up by worms, or dust, in the bony emptiness of her beautifully shaped skull as it rested beneath the earth. I'll admit now with full candor that it was an absurdly grand and arrogant thought. It was the kind of thought (I thought) that you could only have in a train station during the holiday season with a beautiful young person across from you who had just signed away whatever secrets you might bestow upon them. It was the kind of thought that brought fire to the mind—for a few seconds—and then fell away into the category of that which is absurd but at the same time true. It was the kind of thought, I thought, that Andrew Wyeth might have had at dawn, as he departed his studio with his sketchbook in hand, while the earth gave off a soft roil of steamy vapor that hid the distant hills and seemed to bring the stone walls closer as he took it all in, feeling honestly established in that landscape, with a sense of agency (a word, I admit, he'd never use), full ownership that came from his ability to paint it in his own manner. It was Andrew Wyeth's thought and my thought at the same time, as I turned back to the business at hand—my own voice growing authoritative and firm—and went into the finer details of what I'd expect from her as my assistant in the year to come, explaining again, at the risk of redundancy, how rumors might get out, free-floating, shape-shifting, eager to form the perfect case against me as they pass from mind to mind.

# FIRST ENCOUNTER

guess I'm just thinking about the funeral. I'm thinking about how I still can't remember seeing Marsha after she left the car, or even being aware of her presence in any way," I said. More than a year had passed, and at that time we were still rehashing the tragedy.

On the bed Irene was up and over me, gazing intently with eyes grayer than usual, scrutinizing, as if looking for a clue. It was a look I'll never forget.

"I'm thinking about how I know she was there, suffering in hell, but for me she wasn't there. If that makes any sense," I said.

"Maybe you just, well, maybe you were just too, maybe you avoided her." Irene spoke softly and carefully, as if gathering each word. "Maybe it was too much for you to take, the pain you knew she was in. Or maybe—now that some time has passed—you just put it aside."

"Put it aside," I said.

"Put it aside."

"Forgot about it."

"Yes, forgot it because it was too painful."

Another gust of wind came in from the Atlantic and swept over the Cape. On the day after Thanksgiving the streets were empty except for a few locals tearing from one place to another at exorbitant speeds, freed up from the summer bustle, like dogs loose from the leash.

"Maybe," I said. I could remember searching carefully for my daughter at the graveside. I saw her leave the car, an unlit cigarette in her mouth, a pair of Converse All Stars peeking out from under her long black dress. I could remember Frank's father consumed with grief, dressed in a trench coat, standing in the rain staring down the hill and out at the river. A drunk, he'd bought a half share of a failing gas station just off the last exit before the bridge. I felt for the guy. He suffered from chronic pain—he'd broken many, many toes. Now his son was dead from a car collision up near West Point. The casket was lowered into the ground. It splashed when it hit the bottom. A few words about Jesus were mumbled. So much for purity! So much for youth! The funeral parlor had loaned us a black sedan. It felt unseemly to follow the dead kid in our minivan, which had a long sideswipe along the driver's side.

Here's the way I thought about it at the time: loss creates a void, and the void is often filled with drugs. The loss could be anything—parents recently divorced, a good friend moved away, a boyfriend killed on a cold, wet night the way Frank was, taking a curve too fast along 9D. The same stretch of road used for a Mercedes-Benz commercial—one that aired every night during the evening news. A downward spiral began—grades dropped, calls arrived from Mr. Silverstein, the guidance counselor at the high school. "Mr. Walk, your daughter seems to be making a point of avoiding algebra in particular," he said. "As a matter of fact, she seems to be making a point of missing just about all of her classes, with the exception of English."

To catch her at it, to take hold of her shoulders and shake some sense into her in a traditional, fatherly manner would make all the difference, I believed. A few days later I gave Silverstein a call and asked him to peek in on her. "I'm afraid she's not present," he reported back.

"Not present?"

"Not here."

"Not here?"

"Not present."

I drove to Look Park, across from the school. Look Park was sort of a wildlife preserve for truants. Fuckups wandered the grounds in herds, hid not behind but actually inside evergreen bushes, swam in the stream, and taunted the golfers teeing off on the western border. I found her asleep with her arms spread out over the rough boards of an old picnic table. Down by the duck pond her friends kept toking. The smell of smoke drifting between the willow fronds . . . Ah, sweet pot of youth, I thought, while the other, fatherly part, of course, was appalled at this flaunting of illegal substances in my presence. I had to shake her awake. Two tiny pricks of black, her pupils. With a fireman's carry, I lugged her to the car. In the same manner, I dragged her into the house and set her on the sofa and drew a blanket to her chin.

"I rescued you," I said when she woke up.

"You did?" She shook her head, shook it hard, then again, violently, leaning over the edge of the cushions.

"Something's stuck," she was saying. Her tone was serious and soft. "I feel it. There's something in my head. Something's stuck." (Still shaking her head, rotating it on her neck.) "Now it's loose. It's like a piece of glass. I hear it. Do you hear it? More like metal. There's a loose bolt. I hear it, a loose bolt in my head. I hear it. I do. Do you hear it? I hear the bolt. Daddy, there's a loose bolt in my skull."

Then she was seized by an electric jolt that almost sent her to the floor. Dr. Lewis explained later that it had been a seizure. Blood tests showed traces of unidentifiable toxins.

"I wish I could be more exact," Dr. Lewis said, "but certainly pot and cocaine, perhaps opiates."

"Perhaps opiates?"

"Perhaps."

"Perhaps?"

"Perhaps."

"There she was having a seizure on our living room sofa. It was horrible," I was saying. We were in the storage closet, jammed with reams of copy paper and towers of foam cups. Willow covered rental units at our agency. I admired her ability to manage large, uncontrollable numbers; to lure the unsuspecting; and at the same time to maintain the moral high ground. She never lied, exactly. She never pushed, much. She was firm and resolute and wore dark red lipstick in an old-fashioned manner, as if two butterflies were mating on her mouth.

"That's so, so sad," she said, letting her weight fall slightly so that I felt an obligation. We made little adjustments from side to side against the metal shelving unit and began what became a long kiss and then, a few hours later, in my car at the scenic lookout on the parkway, continued. We were all over each other for a few minutes, until I started talking about the seizure again, and she pushed me away, stepped out of the car, and went to the edge of the Palisades, mounting the small steps to the tourist binoculars. I followed her up and fed a quarter into the pedestal. She made a careful surveillance of Riverdale, scanning slowly as if through a submarine periscope, giving her assessments of the properties she saw there, the white towers, the fine estates along the river. She spoke bluntly of her plan to move to a firm that handled that arena. "It's big-time over there," she said. "What with the retirees from the Upper East Side. It's knee-jerk for them. Get old. Move to Riverdale. It's easy money."

When the timer ran out and the shutter slid down, she turned and looked at me and, I guess, recalled the original impetus of our desire, the sadness and loss. "I'm so, so sorry," she said again, leaning to kiss me.

A month after Frank was killed, another kid at Marsha's school died—and three were hospitalized—after smoking jimson weed they'd picked along the edge of the parking lot. By then we'd checked Marsha into a hospital in Westchester, a place up in the hills, with a view of the river.

"You're a lucky man," Dr. Lewis said to me in the hall one afternoon. He was thin and young and moved with an inefficiency that revealed his inexperience. He didn't seem to know how to put his hands in his pockets, to make full use of his white coat. On his upper lip was a small yellow mustache; on his flat chin, a second growth shaped like an arrowhead.

"My point is," he said, "that in a way you were lucky, I mean, if she hadn't had the seizure in the first place, we wouldn't have been able to check her in." He reached up and gave his chip of hair a soft twist, and then, tilting his head slightly, he said, "You have a sweet daughter, Mr. Walk, and I'm certain that she's going to pull through and maintain."

"How old are you? If you don't mind my asking," I said.

"Excuse me, sir?"

"When the Beatles broke big, how old were you?"

"I don't think it would be appropriate for me to comment on the Beatles."

"I was thinking about jimson weed," I said on the bed up at the Cape that afternoon. The wind was still blowing outside, coming in long gusts from the ocean. Irene was still on her elbows gazing down at me, and there was still that scrutinizing look in her eyes. A truck raced by on the road, leaving a trail of muffler noise.

"I was thinking about those kids and wondering what

compelled them to grind up something like that and try to smoke it. Then I realized that when I was a kid we did the exact same kind of thing." I gazed back. It was easy because what I said was truthful. I reached up and touched her hair as a gesture of gratitude, pulling the strands from her face. We had been together for twenty years. We were deep in our marriage. We were still in the struggle of our lives, and we both knew it. Irene was a tender person, but strong and clear-sighted, too. She didn't put up with shit. Her father had worked at an optical factory in Cleveland, grinding glass down into lenses. She worked as a physical therapist, fixing jocks, mostly, people with neck problems, bad knees.

On the bed I started thinking about the lemon-scented model glue I'd used as a kid, stuff that was supposedly non-toxic. It didn't work at all, that safe glue, and I convinced my father to let me buy regular glue, with its nice, calming chemical smell. I got high building models and then, later, with paper bags, during the long, boring Midwestern afternoons near the railroad yard, with my buddies, we huffed and the sky cleared and my brain went to a new kind of heaven that I couldn't forget. That was part of me, I was thinking, looking up at Irene. She knew that part of me. Believe me, she knew.

"Yeah, you did the same," she said. She sat up and smoothed the sides of her dress and stood.

"Yeah."

"Let's go for a walk," she said, moving for the door.

Outside, it had begun to rain.

---

Downstairs in the recliner, staring at the television, legs tucked up, my daughter gave us a suspicious, what-were-you-doing-upstairs-in-the-middle-of-the-afternoon glance. Her fragility was more apparent in the big chair. Her eyes were empty of their former, drug-induced vitality, which had given way initially to a glassy, grief-charged gaze, and then to the flat soberness of someone just barely able to handle reality. She'd taken to wearing woven bracelets of leather around both wrists, in addition to hoops of silver and gold— not one or two but ten or twenty. Moving, she jingled. I still remember that sound.

As Irene rummaged for our foul-weather gear Marsha gave me another kind of look, a mysterious, knowing smile. Then she lifted her finger and pointed at me. I pointed back and nodded. I'll never forget that moment. What were we saying to each other? I can't really say. But it wasn't nice.

"There aren't sea lions this time of year," she said from the chair.

I sensed in the slight rearrangement of her legs that she would, in a matter of seconds, rise slowly, slide into her coat, and pull on her bright red fleece cap with the earflaps that made her look like a World War II aviator.

And she did rise. Crossing slowly to the closet.

This was how we moved as a family unit—a kind of half-hearted, preprogrammed sequence.

Frank had talked to me at times about reading James Joyce in his English class. He especially liked *Dubliners*. He told me of his own Irish roots. The story—true or not, I'll never know—was that his father's father had been a big shot in the IRA. Before that, a few of his ancestors had starved to death in the potato famine. When the boy—and he really was still a boy—was lowered into the ground some deeply secretive part of me, the father part, in an even more secretive way, was relieved. In the months before the accident a foolish, precocious kind of dialogue had developed between him and Marsha, talk of a trip around Europe after graduation, a gap year. I didn't like the idea of a future for my daughter with that boy any more than I liked the idea of what they were doing down in the dim light, on the old couch, alone in the basement, giving each other pleasure.

Anyway, this is how it was, three weeks after the seizure: white corridors lined with fluorescent tubes set into crystalline boxes; and on the walls, bulletin boards stuck with flyers. Willow was waiting for me in her car, parked at the far edge of the lot on the off chance that Irene might swing by the hospital. A burst of wind slipped down the hall, setting all that paper alive: announcements of wilderness workshops, sober houses, suicide hotlines. If I'd been paying attention I'd have heard my wife's voice on that wind, amid the rustle, as she spoke to the reception clerk while he issued her a visitor's tag. Instead I tapped once on Marsha's door and went in to find her alone, in bed, staring vacantly up at the ceiling.

"I saw you," she said. "I saw you kissing that girl from your office."

"Wait," I said. "Wait. Wait. Just wait. Hold on." I moved

to the window and could see—through the chicken-wire glass—the parking lot and the trees; and beyond the trees, the river. Over it the sky held aloft a few feeble clouds and what looked to be the vapor trail of a jet. The vapor trail had that hopeless quality, broken up, slack, like an abandoned whip.

"I'm going to inform Mom of your insincerity," she said. Her voice was sedated, and when I spoke mine was, too.

"No, please."

"It is my duty to bring honesty into the world," she said. "I've been told, here, that I must be an emissary from the world of honesty and truth, to the world of falsehood and lies. Therefore, I'm going to tell Mom."

With that she closed her eyes and seemed to fall asleep.

Then Irene appeared, patting her tag, smoothing her sweater. "Tell me what?"

"Nothing. Nothing," I said. "I think she's talking in her sleep. Could that be a side effect of the medication?"

"Shouldn't be," Irene said. She went to the bed and sat carefully, so as not to wake our daughter. I tried not to notice the elegance of her fingers as they reached for Marsha's brow, touched it lightly, and then pulled the sheet taut and straight. I tried not to watch as she checked the chart, folding the first page back. Irene had been a nurse in Cleveland when we met, before she transitioned to PT. She tapped her finger on some bit of the doctor's scrawl and glanced at me, then back at the scrawl, then at me again, and then—with a sigh—she returned the clipboard to its hook. I told her I had to go see a client in White Plains, and she nodded absently, her eyes on our daughter's placid face. I walked along the hall to the recreation room and stood for a moment.

As far as I'm concerned now, it was luck or the meds. The meds might have played a role in my salvation at that point, swirling what Marsha had seen into the realm of delusion. I liked to think about it that way. I regret that. When she woke, with Irene sleeping in a chair beside the bed, the only thing my daughter said to my wife was, "I saw something strange, Mom. I mean, I had this weird kind of vision."

A few weeks later we made a big event out of picking her up at the hospital. A huge show of bringing her home to her friends, minus the identifiable drug users, and a party with balloons tied to chairs, and a cake that Irene had bought, with a marred frosting job, the letters spelling WELCOME HACK. In champagne glasses filled with cider, bubbles rose in mock solemnity. The nature of these friends became apparent when Marsha broke into tears and they tried to offer their support, a gawky consolation, and then formed a huddle around her and swayed slightly and began to laugh and giggle in a way that made me nervous. They found it impossible to locate the proper words. It wasn't in them. (Irene shared this thought. She and I stayed up late that night talking quietly, hearing the trains passing along the bank of the river, struggling to understand what we were doing wrong, what we were doing right. We went through the details.) After the hug they dove into the food, holding their forks in strange, clawlike grips. When the eating was done my daughter tried the best she could to move the gathering toward some formality, something away and apart from the foul language and the chaos. She rose from her chair and said, "I'd like to toast, like, not only you guys but, like, Frank, too, who's not here but is still here in spirit, because, like, Frank would've been happy about all this, you guys. And I'd like to toast my mom, too, for sticking with me, for being there."

Backing out of the driveway on the Cape, the windshield wipers swapping away, with my daughter in the back seat, for some reason I worried that she might suddenly start talking about seeing that kiss in the hospital parking lot. My worry, I now speculate, came from her suffering, and the drugs used to cure her suffering, and the fact that they'd combined to give me my second chance. Any way you looked at it my reasoning was odious. I turned right on Old Pond Road.

The pond itself was flat and cold, like a giant steel coin. To me all the Cape's kettle ponds had this awkward, out-of-place aspect, dwarfed as they were by the ocean on one side and the bay on the other. This pond had a steep drop-off, from sandy slope to sudden depth. I remember one summer, long ago, holding Marsha, her skinny legs in my arms, and walking her into that water, and then the shock as we both went under. I scrambled back to the sand, raising her aloft, above the surface, and she was crying; and I think, looking back, perhaps that was my first glimpse into the terror of fatherhood, the truth of the matter: I could only do so much to protect her.

By the time we reached First Encounter Beach the rain had subsided to a mist. Every Thanksgiving we hiked the narrow path up to the chunk of granite commemorating the site of the first encounter between Native Americans and Pilgrims. Sheer guesswork, I thought, pulling into the lot. I had the same thought each year, imagining members of the Provincetown Tercentenary Commission wandering around, poking through the dunes, trying to settle on the spot. Then, by virtue of the granite and the plaque, it became the *exact* spot. I thought, too, about the Pilgrims feeding campfires, trying to stay alive, and starvation, fever, murder, all that bloodshed, all that death.

Marsha had been a baby when we first came. We'd walked up the trail on a brilliant fall day to have a picnic at the marker. We picnicked a lot back then. Our new life had been full of quiet moments together. Where had all that beauty gone, all that joy? When I thought of beauty while my daughter was in the hospital, I thought strangely of her arm and of the needle that delivered the meds into her system. Dr. Lewis had explained the process in a soft voice, enumerating the drugs, the names of which I immediately forgot as they all sounded alike to me—Zaband and Zoareloff and Zoack—like characters in a psychedelic Greek myth; but I remember the strange beauty of that needle in her arm, and the small bit of tape over it.

They were ahead of me, around the curve. I could just hear Irene shouting, her voice small on the wind but urgent.

I found her kneeling over Marsha, who was, clearly, having another seizure.

I dialed 911, told the dispatcher where we were. She sounded familiar. "Stay where you are," she said, or something like that. "Do not attempt to move her. Keep her warm."

A few minutes later the ambulance roared into the empty lot, circled the long way around, ignoring us, following the arrows as if unsure where the emergency might be. The EMS guy took her pulse, and she smiled up at him. Then she smiled at me and opened her mouth and whispered something. I leaned down and said, "What, what is it?" She said something that sounded like *see*, as in *See, I'm okay. See, I'm still here. See, this is how it all comes down. See, this is what happens when we betray the truth.*

Let me backtrack here. I have nothing to lose because I have lost everything—the house, the one out there on the Cape, and the one in Irvington, too, and Irene's love, of course, and even, in some ways, Marsha's, although we still talk on the phone every week and sometimes I get a text from her, a smiley-face emoji. I've been told my story doesn't have the tension it needs. It seems it would be better if there'd been more suspicion on Irene's part, or on Marsha's part, or if I'd avoided the highly clichéd fling with Willow. I was over at my buddy Al's house the other day. We were drinking gin on his back porch and smoking cigars, and I began talking over my life and he stopped me and said that he didn't want to hear a fucking sob story. But another time, a few years after all this, when I was dating someone and trying to explain it to her, she said that Irene sounded coldhearted, and that isn't the truth at all. You can go ahead and think I'm trying to cover my ass, but the truth is that Irene was a wonderful person with a massive heart. She'd trained as a physical therapist in part because, growing up, she'd had a sister with a bone disease, and Irene had spent her youth—this was in Ohio—tending to her. She knew how to look at you, to really look, and she knew how to listen. I wish I could put a better spin on what I did, on who I was. I wish a better story were available. When you're outside a marriage peering in—as you always are, hearing an account like this—you've got to keep digging, backtracking, trying to imagine more. For example, the image at the beginning, with Irene leaning over me, gives only part of the scene. Just before that, we'd made love—quietly, trying not to squeak the bed, with Marsha downstairs—and then dressed, as Irene told me about a client who'd relayed to her his own sob story. He lived up near Harriman, not far from Bear Mountain, and he was driving back from Manhattan one night, coming home late, when a deer jumped in front of his car and came through the windshield. (The resulting crash was the cause of his neck problems, which were the reason for his appointment with Irene.) Along the side of the road, with blood streaming down his face, he and the deer, still alive, had communed together—that's the word Irene said he'd used. The man thought he was dying, and the deer, with its big eyes, *was* dying, and the two of them lay in the dark on a summer night. According to Irene, the man said—while she massaged his neck and shoulders—that he'd talked to the deer, confessed everything, and she'd laughed at that and asked him what he'd confessed, and he told her, in an even voice, that he had a separate family, an entire family, the complete package, somewhere else upstate. He was living a double life, like something out of a movie. He'd rolled over then, and Irene had stepped back, as he looked different, his eyes scary. "For God's sake, I'm just kidding," he'd said, laughing, perhaps recognizing the alarm in her expression. "I didn't confess a fucking thing. I don't have a secret family upstate. I can barely handle my own. I just lay there while the deer died."

What can I say? That's all you're left with in the end, I guess. I live in New Mexico now, and when I get up early to run the air is usually cold—desert cold—and dry. The stars are still out, the sprinklers thwapping on the lawns.

"Did she take something?" the EMS guy was asking me as he wheeled the gurney through the lot. "What did she take?" The answer came almost instantly, from his partner, who searched her pockets and extracted a baggie containing several red pills.

I could only watch as they counted to three and slid her into the ambulance. An oxygen mask compressed her features, misted with her exhalations. Something beeped a staccato rhythm.

At the hospital in Hyannis the doctor on her case was old and formal, with silver hair neatly framing one of those handsome faces that only improve as they weather. His demeanor was New England country all the way, a Robert Frost of the medical world, with a hard-bitten manner that seemed born out of rocky soil and stone walls and leaning birches and all of that. He treated us kindly, touching his tie, knotted in a huge four-in-hand against his Adam's apple.

The pills in her pocket were simply an over-the-counter antihistamine and acetaminophen, he explained, a daytime-relief formula, which—in combination with her antidepressants—might have produced an adverse reaction. "Until we get her blood work, that's my best guess," he said. He shook our hands cordially and left us alone with our daughter.

"I saw him," she said when she woke up. "Frank was here." Then she elaborated—her voice barely audible, we leaned down to listen—that Frank had sideburns now, and his hair was even longer than before. As she closed her eyes and drifted back to sleep we went into the hall, where Irene began to cry again, leaning into me. The sound she made rose and fell in modulation, a wobbling that reminded me of a theremin, and in turn of Brian Wilson's innovative use of that instrument on *Pet Sounds*, a record we'd dance around the house to when Marsha was little, wearing her red tights and her plaid skirt, a dancing kid with skinny joints and a big voice taking center stage, using a fireplace tool for a microphone. I sank into that memory, and when I came out of it Irene was staring at me, wiping her eyes.

It was still windy when Marsha was released, but the rain and mist had lifted.

"Frank said to say hello," she said in the car. I looked in the rearview and saw an open, youthful face—happy for once. "He made me promise to give you his love." The colorless flatness in her voice over the last few months had dissipated like the weather.

I suggested that we swing by Marconi Beach for a breath of air. I didn't want to go back to the house yet, not when she was so bright and alive. Of all of the places on the Cape, Marconi was our favorite, not the beach itself but the humble visitor center with the model of Marconi's radio towers, the same ones that had, generations ago, picked up the distress calls from the *Titanic*. It held meaning for us, as a family; we touched base with it each time we came for a holiday.

My idea was to walk up to the little wooden lookout set amid that vast landscape—the miles of dune grass and pines and the infinite sea—and then make a frank confession of my infidelity. Lame as it sounds now, I believed at that moment, behind the wheel of the car, that whatever I might say would be dwarfed by the huge natural forces: the waves smashing into the edge of the continent, the wind howling over the bluffs. That's how I thought back then.

In the open air we'd cry and grieve over everything at once. Irene would understand. Marsha would regain clarity. I would be free of it all. We'd find forgiveness. We'd work through a rough patch. We'd continue on together.

Again they took off ahead of me, arm in arm, tilting slightly into the roar of the wind. Gale warnings were posted for the entire Cape, as a nor'easter hunched along the coast. Above the foam and chop two or three gulls called to one another, diving and swooping on the gusts. The horizon seemed to hold itself low and wary with pre-storm unease. I leaned against the car, waiting, until they were over the ridge, and then began to follow, turning away from the weather to take a breath. Later I'd remember how their jackets, Irene's blue and Marsha's red, contrasted with the gray sky. I'd remember how small they looked, and how I'd been unable to comprehend their strange movements, a kind of jitterbug of anguish as they shifted back and forth—less a hug than a struggle, a wrestling match, a mother-daughter rope-a-dope. I began to run down the path. I ran with my heart pounding like a fist. When I reached them I tried to pull them apart, but they went tumbling to the side. I saw the terrible fright in the corners of Irene's mouth.

"How could you?" she said.

"How could I what?"

"How could you?"

Every word after that, all the words, were blown away by the wind and our grief. My wife and daughter had relaxed their grip but still lay against one another, in the sand and seagrass. I'll never know what was said between them, what it was that made them go into that tangle, but I like to believe that Irene pushed away from the facts, refused to accept what she was hearing. I like to believe, too, that Marsha was clear and persuasive, honest. I backed away a few steps, and then a few more, and then I retreated up the path. At the top of the ridge I stopped and turned and saw them down below, clad in blue and red, brushing the sand from their legs, holding each other up. They would walk close to the edge, stand where the land gave way and crumbled down, see the small bolts set in concrete that were all that remained of the towers, and they would listen as they always did, just briefly, for the last ghostly residue of the SOS signal (*Because, Daddy, nothing ever goes away, really, all those radio waves are still floating out there in endless space, right?*), or the whine of the wind over the guylines, a small shard of sound still echoing from an expired era. A single gull was calling softly to the sea for a companion, for an answer, for anything. And as I returned to the parking lot I was surprised to find the cloud cover suddenly part, and to see someone who looked like Frank, leaning against his car, his red hair afire with the sinking sun.

# STOPPING DISTANCE

## GRIEF AND TIME

Grief takes as long as it wants, in various formations, and doesn't follow rules the way we'd like to think it does. And for God's sake, it doesn't pass through stages. Forget stages, I hate that idea, she said to her friend Valery, who had suggested she try attending a bereavement group. They were walking together on a cloudy afternoon, following a path along the river, with the train tracks up the hill to their right and the river, gray and seething in the fall wind, to their left. Valery, who had gone through a number of steps to get sober and had attended such group meetings with ritualistic, almost religious fervor, seemed absurdly small in her devotion to the therapeutic nature of storytelling, of confession.

## ACROSS THE THRESHOLD

In the group there was a man who lost his teenage daughter two years ago, chasing a Frisbee into the road. It's a cliché and we warn and warn but that's how it happened, he said. It was a warm July afternoon and I was out back—this was my old house, the one I sold last year—on the deck doing some work, and she and her friends were out front, playing, and I could hear them laughing, not giggling but teenage laughs, hoots, shouts, stuff like that. It was a sound I could've listened to forever until that day, and now, of course, I can't stand it. Hearing teenage kids kills me now, he said, and then there was a crushing silence as the group members leaned forward, faces in hands, waiting the expected few seconds for what they knew was coming, the choke of it, the restrictive collapse into sobs. It didn't matter that two years had passed for this man because for a split second—with the gurgle of the coffee maker on the table behind them—those sounds were in the here and now, as he put it when he got his speaking voice back, clearing his throat, his words full of sorrow. His name was Cal and she'd later learn that he lived in Westchester, in Bedford to be exact, in a house in the wooded countryside along a curvy road, with split-rail fences and a white gravel drive. Later she'd sit alongside him in the car outside his house on a clear winter night, with the stars bright overhead and snow windblown across the road, and they'd hear in the music on the radio—something by Chopin, one of the nocturnes, the C-sharp minor, sad and quiet yet somehow uplifting and joyous too—a reflection of their mutual conditions. Something in the formal way he held the steering wheel high, lightly, wiggling his fingers, told her that he would turn and kiss her, and then he'd wait a few seconds and drive up to the house, to delay the weight that would come when they crossed the threshold.

Perhaps she knew in the car that he'd gallantly let her go ahead of him, pushing the door, opening his palms, and tossing his fingers into the air as if to say "after me," and then he'd come in with the rush of cold air—there was wood smoke along with the smell of pine sap—and they'd stand awkwardly for a moment. A sprig of mistletoe would be hanging from a light fixture in the foyer. He'd look up at it and grimace. Ignore that, he'd say, and he did say.

## THE LAWYER

His daughter's name was Drew—like Drew Barrymore, he told them—and he had been unable to say it for over a year, through a bitter divorce and the fury of guilt, until finally one afternoon at the country club, sitting with friends watching kids splash one another in the pool, listening to the laughter, he said her name, Drew, and then said it again. The club didn't want him as a member anymore, not only because he'd been negligent in attending social gatherings, avoided serving on any committees, and refused to golf, but mainly because he'd become a sad sack who had once been a facilitator, a gregarious guy who could talk about anything to anyone in a friendly manner, a person who, as they used to say, got things done and was well liked. Now he was an isolate, quiet and brusque, shrouded in sorrow. He knew it. The members of the club knew it. Yeah, he said, *brusque* is the word I'd use. I snapped when I felt like snapping. I felt, and I still feel, he said to the group, that the structures around my everyday actions, the small, silly fucking rules that make up everyday decorum for the living, polite inquisitions about how it's going, small gestures like a handshake or a pat on the back or whatever, simply no longer mattered. So I just did what I wanted to do, and I still do, when I wanted to do it and when I want to do it, and I said what I wanted to say when I wanted to say it, and still do, in honor of Drew, who would've fucking liked seeing me become a kind of rebel, a punk, he said. And then, after someone else had a turn to speak, he put his hands out and added that he meant to say that he often felt he should approach the world as his daughter had approached it, from an angry fifteen-year-old's vantage. Then he sobbed, and the sob passed gently from one to the other and they all admitted—clutching coffee cups, rubbing their faces—that they were totally helpless, even this far along. For a moment there was a communal flash of grace in the silence, just before someone moaned, or sniffed, or coughed—and the cars outside passed with a judgmental shush that made everyone in the group aware that inside those cars, people were passing with the bitter solace and mindlessness of those who do not know, who have not shared this kind of loss, and in doing so, in passing, were casting a judgment on those inside the church basement, in the chairs, and it was manifested in the sound the tires made as they rotated through the slush.

### GROUP

Grief comes unevenly, not only in relation to the way the bereaved suffers, unique to each personality, but also in relation to the time through which the pain moves, so that for some, a year is more than enough time, or at least adequate, to return to a semblance of normalcy, whereas for others a year is a blip, a flick, a blink, not enough. Other factors—and they all admitted this, talked about it—include the precise manner of your loss, the horrific but necessary circumstances examined over and over again. Jodi, who lost her daughter five years ago in a car crash on the Merritt Parkway, talked obsessively about the need for guardrails on that stretch, about the dangerous nature of decorative trees along the roadside, and, mostly, about the television newscast, the way the information (not news, she cried) had been reported (and I watched, she said, I had to see it, I didn't believe it), the smirk on the announcer's mouth, a man named Greg Gunwald, a square-jawed sportscaster who sat in for the news that night, she said. A man who saw life as a matter of scores, of yards gained and all of that. I could hear it in the way he said, Four teenagers were killed tonight, stressing the word *four* and then putting an even heavier stress on the word *horrific*, the same way he'd stress the word *terrific*, as in the way he'd say the Yankees had a terrific comeback.

## SAILING

Howard lost his son, Andy, in a boating accident, a freak accident, he said again and again, always working in the word *freak*, making sure it was clear that it had been a bright, sunny day on the river near Croton, that little inlet, and that his son had been a highly proficient sailor. The kid had wild golden hair (he said another time, passing the photo around), and then they had waited for the catch in his throat—two years had passed for him, too—but instead his voice grew shrill. He was coming about in high winds, maybe trying a chicken jibe. It was that simple, he said. According to his friend in the boat, he even announced it, sticking with proper protocol. Prepare to come about, he said, and his friends in the boat ducked but he didn't duck low enough and the boom knocked him out of the boat. (It went unspoken, but each one of them in the circle thought about the currents of the river, the tidal complexity of the salt water coming up from the sea, and they all thought about the yearly accidents, the canoes tipped, or those who decided to take a dip unaware of the dangers.) A full sail. The luff along the edges, the abundance of wind along the reach of the river, the arch and tip of the boat in relation to the air and the water; a boy, one hand on his tiller, the other on the main sheet, ducking down but not far enough.

### FIRST DATE

That's the thing about Howard, Cal said in the car on their first official date, after a movie in Mount Pleasant. It's not that I begrudge him the fact that he struggles. It's the way we all just sort of sit there and let him talk about that kid sailing over and over. I guess what I mean to say, Cal continued, his tone taking on an officious air because he was a lawyer and part of his job was to speak this way, to make opening statements. What I mean to say is I think each of us are inclined to see only into our own grief, so we have to work, use up energy, to move away from our own grief into the grief of others—I mean beyond our trigger mechanisms, oh God, sometimes I hate that phrase—and with

Howard it just doesn't seem worth the effort. Now they were sitting together on the couch in his living room. He stood up, said excuse me, and left her alone for a moment. On the side table next to the couch was a framed photograph of his ex-wife: short, blond, prim, her slim legs in riding breeches, holding a crop, her nose flat, bent slightly to one side in a way that gave her a ragged edge that was all the more attractive, gazing directly at the camera with a joyous aggression, as if daring the future to send her a tragedy. Over her, the sky was richly blue, with the negligent brilliance of another perfect Westchester afternoon. Turning away from the photo, she looked out at the falling snow whirling into the window light. From the kitchen came the clink of ice in glasses, the tap of a bottle against glass, a sound that seemed lonely and isolated until he came out with the drinks, one in each hand, hoisting them gently. He was a tall man, with narrow hips and wide shoulders and premature salt-and-pepper hair cut in layers sweeping away from his high brow. He moved with a tentativeness she appreciated, and when he spoke it was in his voice, too, something that—she would much later come to appreciate—went beyond his grief into the natural ease, a part of himself that had been there before his loss.

## COPING

The way she had coped in the early days—she explained to the group on a cold night in December—was to walk around and imagine her son alongside her, and to speak to him about things as if he were in bodily form, still alive, walking through town, past the pizza parlor, turning right at the corner, past Edward Hopper's house, telling him about how she had been a good dancer back in the seventies, when she would do the disco steps, the line actions, with the mirror ball slicing light into fragments, the entire dance floor becoming sequined with light, and her imaginary son would laugh and tease her and call her old and she'd lift her chin, feeling her cheeks tight, too thin, and she'd laugh and then someone, across the street or approaching from up ahead, would give her the odd look that came from seeing someone talking to the empty air, and she'd feel anger, not shame. On occasion she lashed out, saying, What are you looking at, fucker? I lost my son. Other times she'd hold the anger in and feel her face flush and an ache along her lower back, tingling up into her shoulders. It was physical, she told Cal later. They'd share that together. He'd take her across the yard and into the grove of oaks, a windbreak, the remains of the farm that had been on his land years ago, and he'd put his hands to his sides and look up at the stars and confess that he had done the same thing, not so long ago, in Mount Kisco, walking along and conversing with his daughter, talking to her about copyright, about the nature of the Constitution, about his hope that she'd go to law school, follow in the family footsteps.

## GROUP

During those soft, sudden moments of quiet, the sadness seemed pure and mutual between the group members. Someone would say something and then there would be a gasp, an intake of breath, and then around it a silence that seemed stricken—and it was, it was—with a physical anguish so strong it broke apart differences, the bitterness that often went with a story that was told, as the others took it and reflected upon it and then tried and failed to keep it away from their own stories. Then, for what seemed to be a fleeting few seconds, with the thumping of the steam pipes, they'd become aware that they were simply a small group of folks gathered on old folding chairs in a church along a road not far from the river, with the vaulted stone overhead and, above the arches, in the bell tower, the cast-iron bell that was waiting to be rung, the clapper held in position, the rope hanging limp, plunging down through a hole above the entryway, to be pulled by a church elder or usher during the service, the bell ringing outside, muffled and distant, as the rope slipped up through the hole and then, when it was high enough, the elder reaching up to pull it again, smiling at the pleasure of it like a kid in a schoolyard.

At other times there'd be a trite, acidic taste to the words that were spoken, and each of them would retreat inward and close in on the fact that their own grief was integrated into the individual stories of those who were now gone. Then someone would become so overwhelmed by bitterness, unable to hold back, the barrier of civility slipping away, that they'd strike out with a harsh comment, beyond the pale, as she had done early on during their second meeting when a woman named Ruth went on and on and on about an app called JDate, about trying to find a man who would understand that she was a mother who would never be a mother again. Without thinking, she had looked at Ruth and said, You're dating the dead. That's what you're doing.

## SKIING

We were skiing in Vermont with several friends, renting a place called the Bates Mansion, having a wonderful time, she told the group one night. It was bitter cold and I drove Ross up there in the evening, after school. The air was crystal clear and there was a full moon and we were watching the road, and when we got there we couldn't make it up the driveway because of ice, and he got out and said he'd take care of it. He said that. He said, I'll take care of it, Mom, and he got out of the car and grabbed the rear bumper and began to push, and I was steering the wheel back and forth, spinning the tires, and when I made it up the hill he came running around in front of the car and started dancing with his arms over his head, victorious, and I got out and gave him a hug and we just stood there for a few seconds, our breath puffing clouds, and it was silent and cold and snowing. The two of us on a bitter cold winter night, she said. It was the first time he said something like that to me, and I remember thinking to myself that he would say that to me again and again as I got older, as I needed him in different ways, as he got more and more mature, and with him gone it's like something that was meant to be, I mean that was really meant to be, isn't going to be, she said. The group remained quiet, and Cal, next to her, put his hand gently on her hand and lifted it away, touched her once, not in a creepy way,

just quickly with reassurance, and around them in the basement was the purest sort of silence, until the great iron pipes
of the church's heating system gave a thud and the radia-
tors under the basement windows—leaking cold from the
street—shuddered and hissed.

It was the skiing that brought them together, the pure
coincidence of a commonality between their two losses, as
they'd see it, the miraculous nature of the truth as it related to the stories they told themselves. That's how it was.
Out of the blue, two souls lost in some woods come upon
each other and—at a great distance, barely visible, just
silhouettes—recognize something familiar, a slight limp in
the gait, the shape of a head, and when they get close enough,
before they speak, they begin to laugh because they were
old college roommates, or had worked in the same office
in Chicago years ago. A magical feeling began to appear at
the meetings, beyond conspiracy, beyond luck, that foretold
some aspect of existence, sealing a bond that had not existed
before the chance encounter. After she mentioned skiing in
Vermont he waited a few meetings before he mentioned
his own experience, and he kept it vague, just said they
used to go skiing and then he got choked up and couldn't
speak. (Much later he'd see that in the withholding he had
found some hope; he had foreseen the moment when he
would share it with her away from the others, passing it like
a chalice, sealing the bond that was forming, and he knew it
was only an imagined relationship that had formed, glancing over at her, catching a glimpse of her lovely face: narrow
and austere with thin, pale lips and a high, freckled brow that
seemed enhanced by the way her hair, a brown so deep it

was almost red, was pulled back, charged with winter static, loose and curling around her ears, which, when he got close to her during coffee time, looked small, delicate, shell-like when she leaned forward to take a cup, exposing to him for the first time, as the collar of her shirt tightened against it, the long, delicate elegance of her neck.)

## THE RED HAT

I can't tell you, he'd say later. I can't tell you what I was feeling when I heard you talk about skiing, about your boy pushing the car in the driveway, because we used to take my daughter skiing in Vermont, too, and I remember when I drove them up there, same kind of thing, late at night after a meeting in the city, moon in the sky, and my little girl was asleep in the back—this was when our marriage seemed strong, tight, good—and there was that feeling, I mean I knew I'd remember that moment forever and look back at it. I have the mind of an attorney, I'll admit that much, and it seemed to me, I mean it seems to me now, too, that it was evidence that the world was right, and so when I go back to it now, I mean like you did that night, I was thinking, Carol, when you were speaking, that I feel doubly betrayed—not only by the memory itself and what it once meant to me, but by the fact that I actually put it in some sort of mental file and told myself at that time that it was an evidentiary moment, a moment that proved something, proved I was a good father in a good life in a good car driving a moonlit wintery road in Vermont—and now I see that it proved nothing, he said. They were at a restaurant called the

Red Hat, seated outside on the patio, overlooking the river, thirty miles from his house, and it was midsummer, and the candles flickered in a warm breeze off the water, and Manhattan twenty miles downstream was a quivering glob of light in the heat past the pearled beads of the bridge, and the subject had risen up out of the small talk, out of the easeful laughter, and it made that moment—she'd think much later—somehow even more profound, something they'd both remember as formative.

### DRIVES

Late in the winter they began to meet outside the church after meetings, taking long drives north along Route 9D, following the road along the river until the Bear Mountain Bridge appeared, brightly lit, with small stone shanties holding the ends of its cables, desolate and empty as they crossed it, rounding the traffic circle to the Bear Mountain Inn, where a few cars were parked close to the building but the rest of the parking lot, vast, white with salt, stood empty. He'd slow as they passed the inn and they'd look up at the dark windows and think, both of them, about lovers in bed, resting in postcoital slumber, sleeping deeply after the exhilaration of touch. (Later they'd share this impression, looking back.) They barely spoke during these drives. They weren't on a date. I don't feel like going home yet, she'd say on the sidewalk outside the church, and he'd offer her a drive and they'd go. At Bear Mountain he'd drive to the far end of the parking lot, turn the engine off, and they'd sit and listen to music—classical sometimes, or jazz—and then he'd reach over and touch her shoulder and pull her toward him and kiss her, running his hands up into her hair and around her collar, and he'd smell her and she'd smell him, both inside the protective sense that came from the car cooling down, the leather seats under her wool skirt, the bunch of her stockings around her toes, the sense of her breasts inside her bra, her fingers around his thigh, and then they'd push away from each other and sit back, veering instantly into their own grief, feeling a foolish pleasure in the routine, aware of the immensity of their guilt, the rush of it overpowering, but also aware—they'd both later think—that these drives were part of something larger, a process that included the patrol car that appeared each time, the same cop most likely, swinging his flashlight at them, interrupting their solitude, making them feel like a couple of teenage kids.

### THE EROS OF GRIEF

The fuzz of erotic energy was the strange part. He had lost a daughter and she had lost a son, and somehow those two facts began to form a pattern, a logos. What are the odds of two successful people, two divorcés, two relatively attractive people sitting next to each other in a bereavement group in the basement of a church in Westchester, feeling—as they listened and spoke, as the group descended into a unified sensation of pure loss that, in those moments after someone spoke, also felt like grace, like a sensation of free fall, the sudden jolt of a plane in the middle of a transatlantic flight—a sensual awareness of each other as they sat in the hard chairs, shifting haunches, lifting hands to their cheeks, brushing his five o'clock shadow with the bottom of his palm (she saw him do it out of the corner of her eye), or lifting her chest to take a deep breath and, in doing so, allowing him a glimpse?

What were the odds of two people, lonely and lost, coming up to each other during a coffee break and gently, without provocation, as a kind of mutual gesture, lifting their cups as if in a toast, both of them about to sip at the same time, facing each other, and in the uplifting of their hands and the tension that had formed, sloshing the hot coffee onto the floor at the same time? He had a stylized ungainliness that reminded her of Jimmy Stewart, with a voice to match, an aw-shucks way of disregarding his own seriousness while making himself seem, somehow, even more serious. His grief was serious but he wasn't all that serious, he seemed to be saying with his gestures, sipping and leaning back slightly as he spoke. He asked her where she lived and she told him, and he admitted he'd never been to that side of the river, not once in all his years, except a few times when they drove north on the thruway, and when she asked him where he lived he said not far, in Bedford.

## GEOGRAPHY

Each one of them talked about moving out, changing jobs, shifting their footing. He spoke about moving to Aspen, not only to ski, if he could ever get himself to do it again, but just to be in the crisp mountain air near the edge of the atmosphere, closer to the void of space, the open languor of stars, pristine and pure, sunk deep in a darkness that wasn't darkness at all but a lack of material. In Aspen I might feel something new. Another time he talked about moving back to his hometown in Pennsylvania, where it would at least look okay to remain silent, to avoid too much, too much, too much, he said while the group waited for him to continue. That night the windows were open and it was a warm spring evening, a faint smell of bloom in the air. I could be reticent. Everyone's reticent out there, so I wouldn't stand out. Then he talked about the austere farmhouse his father and mother had, like something from the painting of the farmer and his wife and the pitchfork, joined in holy stoic matrimony against the elemental facts of life, pure and clean, not hidden but not up-front. While the others in the group begin to shift uncomfortably, he went on to speak about the way certain brutalities might be faced by not facing them. In another meeting she talked about moving upstate, to a town called Hudson, which was going through a revival, where everyone was creative and trying to find an orderly but fake (she said *fake*) sense of authenticity. Or better yet, she went on, one of those abandoned upstate towns where she could walk as a stranger and strike up friendly banter from time to time, when she felt like it, a town where the streets had lost their grandeur and would mirror her own sense of loss, where houses sat plump and stately but also rotting and half-gone, and then she went silent while everyone in the group, each one of them, thought about the ideal place where everyone was alive and well.

A few nights later, on a drive through the countryside near his house, she said, I feel just the opposite of what I said in the meeting the other night. There simply isn't a place in the world where I'd feel better. If I see a picket fence I think about the backyard, and if I think about the backyard I think about the way he used to make a run at the pool, one of those plastic wading pools, and how I'd tell him to stop and he'd run anyway, making a sliding drive into the water. If I lived in Hudson—I mean it's like one long street going down a hill—I'd still see the river and think about him that way. That night he drove along the reservoir and they looked out at the water and he told her that the original town of Katonah, the first one, was somewhere beneath the water out there, and they both had the same thought: perhaps that was the place to go live again, and then one of them said it and the other said she was thinking the same thing, and instead of crying they both laughed and then he was making fun of the idea, saying, Yeah, let's go live down there. Better yet, we'll blow up the dam and live in whatever's left, and then they stopped at a diner, pale pink neon tubes around a chrome formation, and had pre-dawn pancakes and coffee together, watching the first frills of light around the trees across the road, feeling at that moment secluded and warm in the booth.

## STOPPING DISTANCE

A year later, when they were skiing in Vermont, he told her about his idea for a group called Stopping Distance. Right after the accident, a part of him, the attorney part, wanted to manifest his grief in some active way, to make a formation out of his loss and to transform the world. So I was thinking of starting a group, or a web page, about fast drivers in relation to pedestrians. You could put in a speed and then find out your stopping distance, because at that time I was totally obsessed with the fact that the car that hit her was going too fast, and that if only the kid driving had been going slower he would've stopped just before he hit her. I kept thinking, over and over, Stopping distance, and for a week or so, I mean, when I was totally glazed over in my sadness, not even close to admitting what had happened, it seemed to make total sense, he said. They were on the lift, almost to the top, in the sudden, clear cold of high altitude, and he felt relieved to leave the bar, to feel his skis touch the ice as the chair swung away behind. Just the icy upper reaches—shrouded in low fog—and the steep initial drop of the slope. He split off at the black diamond while she stayed on the blue trail in a parting that seemed to her, in those initial seconds, before she could think, while he was swooping away into the steep drop-off, with the wildly gorgeous vista opening up around them, to be deeply meaningful. By the time she got to the bottom, sweaty and tired, her ankles aching in the tight bindings, his words were gone, until he appeared a few minutes later, whooping and hissing down out of the trees, emerging suddenly, a crystalline dry shush in his bright blue ski jacket, letting the poles dangle at his sides, heading straight at her at top speed before cutting into a long, wide snowplow stop that sprayed a fantail of snow into the air and, with wonderful precision, swept along beside her with his face wet and pink, and his eyes, when he pulled off his goggles, were startling, glinting gray, as he leaned over for a kiss. That's what I mean by stopping distance, he said. It was right then, she'd later think, that she had felt a perfect sense of the destiny of their lives: he would go one way, down the harder course, and she would go the slightly easier path, along the side of the mountain and down an old logging road—but in the end he would emerge, come to a slide alongside her, and they'd kiss and feel alive in a way that was regenerative and, she thought, full of grace. On the way to the lodge, holding her skis, she was aware that she was putting everything into a single symbolic basket, making way too much of the fact that on the way down the hill, in the exhilaration of movement, in her concentration on her legwork, she had forgotten to think about anything at all except reaching the bottom without a spill.

## RECOURSE

When you're living in a certain kind of loss, the only recourse is to look at events as loaded with symbolic portent, as full of signs and indicators pointing a way out of loss, or to the fact that the loss might never go away; it's that or the sad but pure darkness and depression of no meaning at all. One way or the other, at a sway of extremes so that suddenly, say, in the middle of a dinner party, with the sparkle of light on the silver—polished that afternoon, the grimy gray of the paste drying to white and then rubbed carefully away to reveal the mirrored shine—the flicker of candlelight and the warmth of the faces can at one moment seem joyful and hopeful, and then, a second later, seem utterly trite and absurd, as a guest laughs and lifts his fork to make a point. Later she'd have to sort it out, do her best to see what meant what and how much of her life at that time—the dates with Cal, the dinners, the meetings at the church, and her own work at the school, delegating and going through the motions of being principal, examining test scores, meeting with the superintendent, managing the teaching schedules—had been done with intent, looked at with meaning, and how much of it had been lost in the wash of pain, subsumed, cast away. It was important, she'd later feel, to look back and establish patterns, to trace the complex paths that had somehow led to stability, to the grace of a life with pain but also with love.

One afternoon, moving around the kitchen, preparing a roast for dinner, listening to the television set in the den, where Cal was watching a football game, feeling a settled calm of domesticity, looking out the window at the clouds gathering over the trees, wintry, tinged with a blush of amber around the edges, she felt her sadness as it seemed to fall forever into the placid standstill of the moment and stay there. It was a brief, fleeting sensation. Then there was a jocular shout from the den, football-related, and she glanced back out the window and remembered, years back, watching her son as he played in the yard, swinging a stick around, his body small and isolated as he made jousting gestures in the air, moving gallantly in the purity of his playfulness at that moment, a moment she had known, even then, that day—whenever it was, she couldn't really recall—she would file away and remember forever, just as she, on occasion, would go back to that moment in the yard and the pool, his skin glistening seal-wet, and countless other moments that now felt cataloged, sorted out, slightly stiff around the edges, like index cards that had been fingered soft at the corners, and when she left the sink and went to the den to sit with Cal, holding his hand, she stayed silent, let him remain in the present moment, hooting and shouting at the plays, leaning forward. On the screen the college players were hugging one another, jumping up and down, patting rear ends, and pointing fingers at the sky. When the replay came, she watched the quarterback fall back, protected, back farther, his arm cocked and the ball resting in his hand until he unleashed the pass, which arched high into the stadium lights and found a pair of outstretched arms. She watched as the receiver ran in slow motion, with the ball cradled, into the end zone, lifting it to the heavens as if making an offering, and then collapsed onto his knees. He was crossing himself as she turned and went back into the kitchen.

### DAYS

They moved through days joined by the loss, talking about it obsessively, exchanging intimate details. He told her about the afternoon light coming through the trees as he sat in the backyard in a lawn chair that day, listening to the kids playing out front, and then the odd, rubbery, blunt, sudden sound just before—microseconds, really, but in mental replay, long and drawn-out—the screech of car tires on the summer-hot pavement. She retold the story about the trip to Vermont, seeing her son in the driveway; not so much narrative details—outside of the group setting at the church she seemed to stay away from anything resembling a story— but small things, the way he liked to tie his shoes in a double knot, patting the top of the shoes before standing up again, and the stench of his lacrosse gear that couldn't be washed away (he pieced together these fragments into an image of a young kid who had many superstitions when it came to sports, refusing to wash his gear, tying his shoes in particular knots, wrapping his sticks with tape in a certain way, tying up his nets to his own specifications). He was a star athlete. His name was Ross. He seemed destined for greatness. He was only fifteen, but the details she gave made him seem older and wiser, a kid who had braced himself and matured to adulthood during a horrible divorce, a fatherless kid—she refused to talk at all about her ex-husband—who had to make do. She talked of his broad shoulders and the way he stood straight, with a kind of dignity. Everything she said solidified his view of the boy.

## THE MOVE

She moved to his house in Westchester later that year, packing up her stuff, moving around her son's old room, which she hadn't touched since the accident, feeling a resolve, like an iron bar, plunged into her gut, sitting in the car one last time, looking across the driveway at the house and then at the river, and felt the relief of geographic relocation, having left at least a few of the physical reminders behind. He would drift out to the yard from time to time. She'd look out and see him there, standing alone, looking upward, not so much a ghost or an apparition but a clear memory, something she knew she was creating, pushing his image out there amid the pines that had been denuded in the last big storm, many of the long branches twisted off. At that point, for some reason, her grief seemed cheap, like a bad plot in a bad movie, one more thing that Providence had invented to make the world seem brittle and thin. These appearances were as real as the trees in the wind, as real as the walls of the house. He ran around with his stick, throwing the ball at the elastic net, catching it with a twist of his wrist and throwing it back, stopping once to tie his shoes, patting them, and then, with his shoulders straight, glancing back at the house as if he knew she was watching, and it seemed he continued like that for an hour while she stood at the sink, looking out, she told Cal one afternoon. He nodded and gave her a knowing look, and between them, without a word being spoken, a vapor, an ectoplasm of assurance seemed to form, because this, too, was another aspect of their bond, that they could share these crazy intimacies, claim they were true, without shame. He received her grief and she received his, in whatever form it took.

## THE STORY OF HER MOTHER

Her mother, Ella, had lived alone with her own loss for the last twenty years of her life, in a little house in Cleveland, not far from the airport. She had taken the BRT into the city center to work at a clothing store, and then got a job at an airport newsstand a few years later, ringing up candy bars and bottles of water and newspapers and magazines. Ella had lived in Cleveland most of her life, as had her father, also a Hungarian immigrant, who had joined the navy when he was sixteen, forged his documents, and had come back with a tattoo on his arm and an edge that needed drink.

What do you want to work there for? she had asked her mother one afternoon, sitting in the little kitchen—warm, outdated, with a big white stove and linoleum floor with a pattern of little flowers worn away in two spots close to the sink. A small window over the sink opened to a view of the back parking lot of a busy tavern, where night and day people seemed to linger and smoke and break bottles and, on occasion, usually at night, fight. When her father built the house, the parking lot had been—her mother liked to point out each time she visited, each time she looked out the back screen door—an open field. After arriving from Hungary, her father had built the house by hand, using a kit that was first delivered by railroad and then by truck, lifting the boards, which were printed with numbers. Everything but the brick and mortar and the plumbing, the fixtures, and the stove, he liked to point out, and her mother liked to repeat the story. (That's how we salvage the past, locating the small stories and passing them carefully into the future. Always with the same reverent tone, she thought. But the story of my loss isn't something I want to pass on. The only thing I can pass on is the silence.) All that—the memory of that kitchen in Cleveland and those conversations—was in the past, before her mother died and then, a few years later, her son, but she thought of those particular days—the warmth of the kitchen, the exact smell of the floor wax, something called Future, and then she thought about how her mother's death had, for a while, opened a sense of taking a step forward in the timeline, but then her son died and reconfigured the order, destabilized everything, and in this destabilized state she began to understand her mother in a different way, to see that she, too, had found a way to continue on after her father's sudden death—a job at the airport, an arena of transition, fixed in place behind the counter while others moved around her, taking pleasure in the smallest of tasks, neatening stacks of newspapers, listening to the conversations of others.

I don't mind being out there at the airport, her mother said. For one thing, it gives me something to do, and I need to keep busy, and the money helps, and best of all I get to talk to people, to see them as they arrive, thirsty or in need of a sugar boost. Or they buy one kind of magazine when they're leaving for a flight, and usually buy a newspaper when they arrive. That kind of thing, she said. The sad thing, though, she said another day, is when I go to get something to eat and see an old couple, dressed to the nines for a trip, bags sitting there, not speaking at all, just not talking, and then I want to shake them and say, Speak now, when you can, because there's gonna be a day when you'll wish you'd talked more, or gotten out of your marriage in the first place. There were things you could remember forever about your parents, about those who were gone, she thought, remembering her mother. All she could do was imagine her mother, a prim, tidy older woman with perfect skin—no sun, not a bit of sun, not even once in her life, she liked to claim—that looked powdery even when it wasn't powdered, and pale blue eyes, reaching for a candy bar or a bottle of water, perfectly content, or so she claimed, to be working amid the hubbub. The end of life, whatever you're doing near the end, is what seems to define you, someone named Jill in the group said one night, speaking in her Eastern Seaboard, blue-blooded voice, mimicking Katharine Hepburn, annoyingly precise.

## THE NATURAL DEAD

Grief over the natural death of an older person had a different flavor, of course. Everyone knew that, or thought they did. That's another thing: those who have not had a loss so deep and so tragic can only imagine what it's like, and when they try to imagine, for a fleeting second or two, they do so with a bit of a freakish, superstitious avoidance maneuver, because to go too close to trying to imagine it might be to jinx something so that it becomes a reality of some kind, if not a material reality, an imagined reality. It just can't be done. Those in the group who talked of others often spoke judgmentally of those who had not experienced such pain, as a way of getting a firm footing on the outcrop of their loss. They don't want to think about it. But even when they try, they really don't, someone in the group once said. Perhaps it was Jill, who wore black wool skirts and wonderful shoes, designer shoes with bloodred soles, and stoic black blouses, and, on one occasion, a Jackie Kennedy–style veil. Jill's little boy—from what could be pieced together—had gone through a long fight with cancer, starting at age nine, stretching year after year into his late teens. The anger Jill brought to the group had to be respected and channeled gently away. They listened and nodded, made polite comments about how well she articulated her pain. The men in

the group, at least outwardly, in their gestures, seemed better equipped to understand her rage, the desire to lash out
at those who just didn't, and would never, ever, ever get it.
They pounded fists into fists and nodded in agreement and
said they could totally understand. I've wanted to punch
a doctor myself, Cal said, and then he blushed, spreading
his palms on his knees, leaning forward, and adding, but of
course I wouldn't. I'd get hold of myself. I'd remind myself
of the legal consequences, of course, but I'd also tell myself
that they have nothing to do with it, and can't get it, and
that I have to understand that fact, I mean really understand it, or it will eat me up. (He mentioned his Stopping
Distance project later in that same meeting.) Whereas most
of the women resorted to a series of soft touches, to verbal
diversion techniques (You shouldn't even think about how
other people might be feeling), and to an agreement, silent
and unspoken but visible in their eyes, in their aversion to
what the men had said, that at times all you can do is say
"now now, now now," and hug and hold one another as you
release yourself into the physicality of grief.

## THE WEDDING

The wedding would take place at a church Cal knew in
Garrison, not far from Cold Spring, a small chapel atop a
stone outcrop that he had spotted one morning from the
train, on the way up to file a claim at the federal bank-
ruptcy court in Poughkeepsie. Seen from the train window,
the chapel seemed to float above the river. They would settle
into a comfortable arrangement, move away from his house

in Westchester, find a place new and apart from both of their old lives where they could settle into their twilight years, arranging life around their mutual loss, which would, by that time, be a powerful but manageable pain in the field of memory. He'd retire from his law firm in the city, manage his stocks on a computer screen as a hobby, and get up for coffee in late afternoon. There would be the years of wearing slippers into the afternoon, of moving around the house in a leisurely manner, of making small decisions as if they were big, paging through the Metropolitan Opera brochure, planning the season, picking *La Bohème* and *Boris Godunov*, looking forward to the train ride into Grand Central, the cab over to Lincoln Center. Ahead, they would sense, was the end of the line, a terminus of sorts, so the days would compress, tighten, and there would be a sense of urgency in the way they filled the calendar, a sense of a desire to get as much in as they could while the going was good— she liked to say—of making use of time in a way that was respectful, zeroing in on the abundance of each moment, stopping, from time to time, alone, in the later afternoons, to simply hold each other in the living room, establishing the kind of intense eye contact that occurred between older people, who, after looking back, would make an effort to home in on the present. Then, on some particular afternoon she would feel it between them, the large, abstract silence that was, they both knew, a formation around the unspoken loss, which was not so much a black hole—as she imagined it—as a black speck, whatever was left when enough was forgotten. (Because, as someone said one night in the group, You can't fully remember pain. Pain comes and goes. Physical pain, most of all, but mental pain, too, otherwise you'd never go on. If you remembered what it was like to give birth, if you could recall that pain with acuteness, you'd never do it again, is what I think, someone had said.)

## BINDINGS

And it did turn out that way, for the most part, although a few years after he had resigned from the firm they moved west to a small house in Pennsylvania, not far from the Delaware Water Gap, up on a ridge overlooking the valley, far away from the Hudson River, which had somehow, they admitted, united them symbolically and proved too much to bear, a reminder in too many ways, couched in two different memories, his and hers, but still flowing through the pain. His father had had a hardware business in Stroudsburg, and he went to the shop in the mornings and helped out, sharpening lawn mower blades (at least that was one thing he mentioned doing), holding the metal against the spinning sharpening stone, blowing the dust off, running his thumb along the edge, imagining all the grass it would cut on summer afternoons. For that was another part of it, finding release in the minutiae of daily life, and both of them had longed to get away from what had been the complexity of the city, to find a new ritual. He screened windows, running the rubber band into the groove with a roller, and moved around the shop while his father—unfashionably stoic, hunched over in chronic pain from his arthritic neck, having survived the Depression on a farm in Bismarck, North Dakota—worked at the register. One afternoon,

shortly after his father went into the hospital with conges-
tive heart failure (What's failing? Nothing's goddamn failing, his father had said, frustrated), Cal sat in the back of
the store, amid the goods, with the pale midafternoon light
coming through the front window, down across the old
wooden aisles, barely lit, the feeble neon overhead fixtures
long burned out, and began to cry for the first time in three
years, feeling the waves of anguish arrive, not in response to
any precise stimulus or memory, but simply because of the
way the light looked and the intense silence of the store,
and he recalled, because he groped around, felt a need to
find a source for his grief, to pin it to some particular image, his daughter in her ski gear, stiff in the nylon embrace,
her face puffy, wet, and red—a baby face, the same face she
had as a baby when he lifted her out of the bathtub—as
she stood and waited while he adjusted the tension on her
bindings, twisting the small screw. Right then, on the ski
slope, he thought in the store, he had had a profound insight: to protect his daughter, the tension had to be exactly
right, loose enough so that the skis would fly away under
force but tight enough to sustain her on her run down the
mountain, because she was a shaggy, youthful skier, loose
in the joints, free, fearless, dangerously reckless in a spirited
way. He would explain all of this to Carol later that night,
in bed. I had to find something to make sense of it, he told
her. Otherwise it was just another one of those waves that
come more and more infrequently. Otherwise I was just
this sad old man in the back of a hardware store crying
like a fool. So I thought about the way she used to look
when she came down to the bottom of the mountain, you

know, suddenly appearing. She'd always ski the last run of the day, and she'd always take some back trail, and she'd take as much time as she could, until it was almost dark. And I'd always—and this happened three years in a row—wait for her and worry, worry and wait, and then she'd appear, he explained, and for the first time in three years they wept together, snow falling outside into the valley behind the house, and out there somewhere below, the Delaware River plunged through the ease of the gap.

That's how it worked, he thought. You want nothing more than a straight line away from grief, to disassociate the story from geography, from landscape and the things in the landscape, the shrill morning call of some bird waking before sunrise, startling the early morning dusk, a kid with a skateboard, his feet as if glued, betraying physics as he skips with a jerk up a curbstone. All you want is a semblance of orderly structure in your progression back into the world, while others find it dubious that someone who has lost so much isn't wallowing in the eternal loss, because the entire house, up on the ridge, overlooking the valley on that clear, cold winter night, seemed to be spinning into a whirlpool for a moment as they held each other in bed. Then, just as suddenly, it was over, and he went and turned on the late show, and they watched the opening monologue. You grant yourself the grace of a story, but then it goes away. People spin stories around your loss. The unimaginable is the most fearsome thing. In some small pocket, some primal recess of their minds, some dark little cave, is a place where the deepest fear rests, some assure themselves to feel better. Put it there, they say to themselves, and then they lean down and tie a shoelace on a little foot, or wipe a mouth, or kiss a forehead, or tuck a blanket under a chin, or remove a Band-Aid with a swift, urgent sweep and then laugh it away. Woe to the one who admits that those dark little places, the boxes—he thought the next afternoon, sorting nails, opening and closing the long wooden drawers, enjoying the heft and the rattle—do not exist at all, because when you lose something dear it builds a box that you can't imagine, he thought, and then a customer came in, the bell over the door tinkled, and he went back to moving through reality again, the floor creaking under his shoes, going to the register and saying hello to Marge Pierson, one of his father's favorites, gaunt but still elegant, her eyes deep blue, a former beauty queen, a woman with her own sorrows, a woman who had lost her husband years back in a horrific car accident and still carried it with her somehow, in the scarf she wore around her neck, in the way she clutched her small purse, in the cut of her skirt over her bony hips.

Grief in prepackaged form, he thought, sweeping the back of the shop, thinking about a smart little piece he had seen on the news that morning about a woman who, as a way of overcoming her loss, had formed a fund for children like her daughter. Lilly's Fund. The music began to swell beneath her voice halfway through, and then emerging onto the screen in soft focus was the face of a child, angelic, of course, with downy, windblown hair and eyes that were wide and blue and, of course, deeply innocent, with freckles around her perfect nose, and then, before you could take that image in, they were back in a studio in New York with the mother, who was also somewhat angelic, her face seemingly free of makeup and startlingly assured as she explained that she had set up a fund not as a way to help herself through her loss but as a way to help other kids in the name of her daughter and to assure the world that no one else in the future would have to suffer such a loss. But at that point a shot of her hands appeared, just her hands, folded together in her lap, and he saw in the image of her fingers interlaced that the package she had created meant nothing outside of the context of the production itself, the ads that framed her story, and he thought, and told his wife later that night, that nothing could package grief, not really, not a fund, not anything like his idea, Stopping Distance, nothing at all. He said that and then stopped speaking, another of his non sequiturs arriving out of the blue as they read together in bed, leaning against the headboard side by side, and he said it and she nodded and remained silent, because to say something more—they both knew—would be to open the door to a particular dialogue that, for the most part, was better left unspoken.

What was inside that silence was the fact that the previous candor, the words spoken in the group years back—not so long ago, really, but long enough to seem threadbare—had worked magic at that moment in their lives and was now unnecessary. He was speaking, changing the subject, of his old English professor at Princeton, a man named Shilling, who had taught them about James Joyce, about the idea of epiphany. He had us write our own, or at least attempt one, and I wrote mine about my father, something about him in the house—not that far away from this place here, Carol—and then he let his voice trail off as he remembered the old room, the thick plaster walls and the dormer and the small ledge by the window with the cushion where he used to sit, looking out at the rolling hills, and where he probably sat to write his epiphany on a cold winter night like this one. What had he written about? He couldn't remember, not at all, just that it had some tragic overtone, and it was one of those moments that he thought he would hold forever, just as he thought he'd hold forever the sound of the contact of the car when it hit Drew, the silence that came before it happened and the sudden silence when it was over. But now, he admitted, it was gone. On the bed, he absently reached over and touched her shoulder lightly and let his hand rest there a moment while she read. Then he stood up and went to the window and looked out at a view that was, basically, with only a mile or two of difference, the same one he had seen as a kid. The snow was moving through the wan moonlight, fuzzy and haloed, and beyond the trees at the edge of the yard he could see the faint outline of the Blue Mountains. Yes, the candor of those meetings, the frankness and intensity of confession, the sharing of pain from mouth to mouth had formed a basic physics that purged the details away, and the frank, open talk, it now seemed, had been predicated on the fact of forgetfulness couched, most certainly, in a sense of safety that came not only from their shared loss but also a shared sense that most of what they said, like everything else, would vaporize into the future, disappear. All that would remain—and all that does remain—is the structure of the process, the grace of mutual attention shared for a few hours, once a week, in that basement room that smelled of wood polish and floor wax, with the pipes banging and the sense

that overhead was a sacred space, empty pews and unlit candles and stained-glass windows—vivid by day, with scenes
from the book of Psalms, and a dove in the upper window
with an olive branch in its beak—invisible at night aside
from faint outlines of scenes fused with the dark outside.

Over the years there had been between them a sense of
guilt that appeared from time to time, usually when they
were alone in the car on rare visits back to New York, over
the fact that somehow they had found joy and compan-
ionship and had been brought together by mutual loss, he
thought at the window. But then he was turning away from
the window and standing near the bed, and she looked up
from her book, sensing that he had something important to
say, and he was about to suggest that they fly to Aspen sometime soon, maybe in a couple of weeks, and ski dry powder.
He'd go ahead and test his skills on a black diamond while
she, if she wanted, he'd say—and he did say, a few seconds
later—could, if she felt like it, take the slower back trails,
and then he'd stand at the bottom of the mountain and wait
for her to emerge, the sounds of her skis arriving first, that
magical hiss, and then she would emerge with joy, and she'd
swing around and spray powder in his face, and he'd let it
melt on his cheeks until she reached up to brush it away.

## THE DEPLETION PROMPTS

Write about that night, long ago, when you lay in bed listening to the sound of wind buzzing through the old television aerial mounted on the porch outside your bedroom—remember the door out to the tin roof, the buckle and ting against your toes—a deeply disturbing sound, like a stuck harmonica reed, one that, combined with the sound of crying drifting from downstairs through the heater duct, seemed indicative of more troubling harmonics.

Write about the way that, one summer afternoon, your older sister, Meg, disappeared, heading out into the *beyond*, as you saw it, until finally she called one night in September to explain that she was fine, safe in California, not far from a red-wood forest, staying with a guy named Billy, which caused your father, who was cradling the heavy black phone, the receiver tight against his lips, to grimace tightly—his face bewhiskered, thick with stubble—before he began weeping softly, as he turned and, suddenly, with a grand sweep of his arms, held the phone up and away from him so that the curls of the spiral cord spread out and the mute intonation of the dial tone was audible: remembered years later.

Write about the summer—the dead heart of it—up in northern Michigan, when you wandered alone for days on end, feeling the acute isolation but also relishing the joy of being away from home, far away, although even there, sitting on the shore of the lake, listening to the waves plunge against the stone pier, you were aware that trouble was brewing downstate, where your sister had been caught with an older man. Write about the whispers you heard, your father leaning against the sideboard in the dining room, lifting the glass to his lips, your mother's voice full of anxiety. Use just the whispers, fragments of tense language, to build the fuzzy narrative that you carried, that you conjured as you wandered alone: two shadow figures naked in a bed lit by quartz lamps.

Write about Jerry Green, the neighborhood bully, with his shaggy bangs hanging over his face and the way he swung his head to move his hair and reveal his eyes, riveted and angry, bloodshot, full of a desire for revenge as he pinned you against the fence—the one on the way to school—and dug a single knuckle into your chest and warned you that he was going to kill you. Explore the reasoning behind his threat: something about your older sister, something about something she had done to him, or to other boys, or to her reputation. Do your best to be as specific as possible while also bending around the truth so as to protect the living.

Write about the time a search party was sent out on a winter night to find her, a whole posse of neighborhood men, including Dr. Frank, the allergist who gave you shots, and how, having caught wind of the situation, they gathered in the snow outside the front door like carolers, the lights from the doorway casting their placid, eager faces into masks, and how they went out with your father and searched the frozen lake on snowmobiles, looking for what they thought, or feared at least, would be a body, and then came back to sit at the kitchen table and discuss the matter—your mother's soft cries and their talk traveled up the furnace duct into your room as you leaned over it and listened. Get those words down, the tension and strange eroticism—find a way to name it—of their desire to help out, and the way, later, your sister came home smiling and manic, and laughed at your father's concern.

Write about the strange dynamic between the past and present as the dynamic tries to put itself into words. Write about the failure of language to reclaim pain, and how you tried, again and again, to find a way into the topic like Nabokov did in his story "Signs and Symbols," about an older couple trying to navigate around their mentally ill son. Steal his story—as others have stolen it—and reframe it and re-build using his structure. Go fearlessly and take as much as you want and ease the burden of dreaming up your own structure.

Write about the baby born in a closet somewhere in Michigan, back in the 1970s, and a teenage kid too afraid to let anyone know she was pregnant, hiding it beneath blouses and ponchos, which wasn't hard because those loose tops were the fashion, along with bell-bottoms, and it was perfectly fine to float around as if oblivious, and then she had the baby in the closet. That's the center of the story, that phrase, that idea, huddled back in the dark—terrified—hunched over. Take that image and connect it to the one you saw in Lamaze class on the Upper West Side: everyone on beanbag chairs, watching a video about childbirth, and you saw a woman—in what country?—in a special chair, in a squat position, the baby emerging with what seemed to be ease, the head ballooning out and then the slippery emergence of new life. Connect that image with your sister, too, and then merge them together so that it was her, the sister (not your sister but the one in the story, although there will be that blurry line formed between what you write and what readers project onto the story, of course), so that there is confusion in the narrator's mind, a young boy with a wayward sister. Use that word, *wayward*, to describe the way the young boy thinks about his sister, in his confusion, as he hears—or perhaps imagines—her cries in the afternoon, behind the closet door, and opens it to the sight of her there, her face sweaty and in pain, her hands smeared with blood.

Write about so-called toxic masculinity but try to find stories that triangulate with your sister's story somehow, which shouldn't be too hard because that was the way it worked: no matter what was going on, you saw boys in relation to your sister. Write about how, years later, walking in the East Village with a male friend, someone you were just getting to know, you were horrified when he stopped walking and stood there ogling a woman on the other side of the street, shaking his head. Write about the destabilized sense you had as you continued walking with him, and in the same story jump back to the past and to the experience of being a small boy watching a young man coming to take your sister out, observing him as he pulls up in his car, an old El Dorado, not leaving his place behind the wheel, his hair long, his eyes glassy, giving you a curt little nod and blowing smoke from his cigarette into the air, motioning for your sister to come around to the passenger door. Write about the way she skipped lightly in her halter top. How you looked away and then back, feeling shame and anger.

Write about a mother—your mother!—who is so grief-stricken, so in denial, that she sneaks off to the state mental hospital at night to pay your sister a visit. Make it a warm summer night with insects singing in the bushes, and describe how she goes to the loading dock in the starlight, describe the thick black rubber bumpers where the trucks pull up, behind the ward. As she stands, as she looks beyond the hospital and down the hill, a train horn will enter this scene, and she'll think of trips to Chicago she took with her family as a girl in the 1940s, and how everything back then was related to the war, and how the trains, burning soft coal, blew huge plumes of horrific smoke from their stacks—and then the security guard will appear, catching hold of her shoulder. Describe her confusion and terror as he makes the assumption, naturally, considering her state, the way she's shaking, that she's a patient escaped from lockdown for a cigarette, and how before she knows it she's inside the ward in a Velcro restraining jacket. Describe her revolt. The madness of a mother—your mother—losing her shit and acting insane and then becoming insane. The needle plunging into the thick flesh of her arm. Draw from Chekhov's story "Ward No. 6" so that the mother ends up as a patient in the same ward as the daughter.

Write two versions: happy ending, sad ending. In the happy version she talks her way out of the restraints and explains to a staff person—a younger woman who nods eagerly as she listens—that she is Meg's mother. That she simply wants to see her daughter. There are metal bars on the window and moonlight segments the bars into shadows and she thinks of the old noir movies. In the happy version the guard takes her to see her daughter, leaving the lights out, and she goes to the cot where her daughter sleeps and gently wakes her and they embrace and hold each other. Out near the loading dock, the father pulls up in his car and honks the horn to reclaim his wife. They drive home and sit in the breakfast nook drinking coffee and smoking and talking deep into the night. Near dawn, the phone rings and it's the young female guard, giving an update, saying, Meg is going to get better. She was helped by your appearance last night, she'll say. She'll use that word, *appearance*, and it'll sound off-key, somehow, but you'll leave it in the story anyway.

Write the sad version, in which the mother is restrained and evaluated by the staff. A doctor arrives—mild-mannered, with a crew cut—and writes on a clipboard. At first, it's believed that the mother is a delusional patient with schizoid disorder who has given herself a false identity, so a bed check is conducted to see who might be missing. Someone is missing, because a patient slipped away earlier in the night, sneaking out into the warm darkness stark naked, working her way through the gap in the fence behind the main ward, down through the weeds and grass to the creek bed at the bottom of the hill. She sits in the water and lets it wash over her as she smokes. Eventually, things are sorted out—but it's dawn—and the mother, still restrained, is evaluated by the morning staff and the morning doctor, who finally believes she is, indeed, the mother of Meg Allen, and yet concludes that she, too, is in need of care. When the husband—your father!—arrives, there is conversation with the doctors. String this out for several pages and carefully build the narrative so that we're moving into the father's mind, watching out the window as patients walk the grounds, the green light filtering through the trees outside and falling across the doctor's face, which, when the father turns to look, is kind and thoughtful. Let the father suddenly come to the realization that his wife is ill, too, and also show the reader that this is a dubious claim, and that the story is locked into a time when men conspire against women in this way. Attempt to maintain a subtle balance, so that the reader has to work to tweeze this out; end the scene with the father back in his car, casually lighting a cigar, cracking the windows, listening to the radio as he drives, and enters his future, which will be reflected—in his own eyes, at least—in the beauty of the day, the deep blue cast of the summer sky and the silence of the neighborhood in the heat.

Write at least six versions of the story, using different points of view, until you realize that the one with the sad ending is impossible to finish. Write another version in which the wife is taken home by the husband, curled weeping against the car door.

Write into the steel of your rage, a rage that seems lost to you now as you sit alone in a house during a pandemic, confined to the space not only by your desire to create but also by a desire to stay safe. Write about the city, twenty miles down the river, locked down, the streets silent—the streets of the East Village ghostly quiet—until you feel the rage re-center you, return, and then move from that to find images of your hometown again, of the Michigan winters, snow piling thick on cars, the streets quiet, and then shift the story

back to the summer, back to the family with the daughter
in the hospital. Keep reclaiming the rage you felt. Remember the time you visited your sister in the public housing on
the edge of town—just look at the building, driftwood gray,
the stairway to her apartment rickety, the handrail splintery,
and recall that extremely hot day you drove there, under the
railroad tracks and through the dirty viaduct into the weedy
backside of town, sensing that people there were hidden
from view, part of the great national project of denial—
you thought that, and you'll use that phrase—so that when
you got to her apartment building you sat and considered
it knowingly, removing yourself from the scene to capture
it in your imagination, to store it away for just this kind of
moment. Write into that rage as you try again to capture
the mother, short and overweight, her despair, speaking to
the hospital attendant in a voice that is tight and childish.


Write a story about a bunch of kids on the train tracks
down the hill from your house in Michigan, fucking around
in the rail yard, throwing rocks at the sides of boxcars, fid-
dling with switch locks; three young boys, all angry, and one
has a sister like your own, and somehow, no matter what
kind of trouble he gets into, he triangulates that trouble
with her, sees his own actions and the actions of his friends
in relation to her; walking the little trestle bridge over the
sludge river, the goopy paper pulp gray and thick with a
crust, thinking of his sister somehow in relation to the one
named Jerry, who is bigger, a bully at heart, ahead of him
and the other kid, turning around quickly and threatening

to push someone in if they dare approach, leaving them stranded on the trestle—which isn't that long, really—not daring to move forward or to retreat. His eyes are green, which seems too fantastic considering his last name, Green, but you leave it in, and his mouth is set firm the way it gets just before he becomes violent, and right then on the trestle the boys are aware—or you have a vision, in the story—of the future, of a boy like Jerry and his own sister, so instead of backing off he plunges ahead, making a loud hooting sound, and rushes Jerry with all his might until the bully tumbles to the side and falls, his feet touching the toxic paper-pulp waste, looking up with rage-filled eyes, eyes that could tear you apart. Write into this moment and find the ending, which will include the long trudge back up the hill and entering a kitchen—warm, with the window steamed, the smell of tuna casserole—as if entering another world.

Write by drawing from an obscure story by Nelson Algren, one of his Texas stories about poor folks stealing coal to survive, waiting by the tracks for a train to roll past, scampering up onto the cars and tossing pieces of coal down—or maybe they collect pieces that have dislodged and fallen off the train—and, as they scurry around in their madness for warmth, a little girl is hit by the train, and in the end all that is left in the dirty ballast along the tracks is her Kewpie doll, which becomes the title of the story. Somehow transform this into a story about a sister who isn't the little girl but a young woman who's down in the rail yard, high, with her other fuckup friends, maybe even Jerry—somewhat older—messing around but also somehow trying to save themselves from another kind of coldness, and above them is the Michigan twilight you've used before (go ahead and use the word *eggplant* again) and then it happens and she slips and it is over and she looks like a rag doll; transfer all of your fears as a teenager into that moment in the story, the lost, forlorn eyes, empty of life, staring up into that sky and into your own mind as you write. The fuckup kids, fearfully running away, lifting their legs high as they sprint, running up the hill—the road is still a brick road for some reason—and stopping at the top to huddle, to conspire a story to tell their folks, to cover up what really happened.

Write a story in a strictly confessional tone, allowing the narrator to come out and say, Once upon a time, there was a young man who had a mentally ill sister, and then spell it out in clinical terms and without the fear that writing into the story will somehow burn out your other creative inspirations. Use that as part of the story, writing about creativity and inspiration and how you fear depletion of energies. If it helps, call the story "The Depletion." The confessional tone will—if it works—shroud the fundamental truth of the story itself: that inside any confession there is always a tonal quivering of distaste and distrust, perhaps inside the reader's mind, too. Lean into that and go ahead and describe what it was like, the confusion and loneliness of watching your sister as she howled at night, the windows dark.

————

Write a rant inside the story against the concept of prompts as a tool, as a way to write, and in doing so explain that the prompt itself is always a form of limitation, a matter of forcing the writer into a prefabricated box, into an imitation of some other voice, and express your sense, over the years, of reading stories that were obviously created, sparked, urged on via a prompt. Use as an example the idea of instructions as a prompt, explain that someone—a writer you admire—originally wrote a story (several stories, actually) that took the form of instructions, or how-to (avoid naming her name, for the sake of propriety). And then lament the fact that when you were reading stories by other writers, you couldn't help but feel her prompt lurking offstage—a shadow, maybe even a presence brushing the curtain fabric, revealing a shoulder, or an arm—and breaking the dream apart, although you'll admit in this story that you're too sensitive and prone to grandiosity when it comes to these things, detailing an aesthetic belief system before you let the story peter out into a formality that is horrifically stiff, letting go of any intention at all you might have to tell a story, and leave it at that. Let it go. Admit that you feel out of fuel, that the spark is gone, and that you're sitting alone in a room trying to come up with a way to regain the dream, to find a story, because there is a young woman, your sister, maybe, maybe not, sitting alone on a curb during a pandemic, her face wrapped in a blue bandanna, or scarf. The streets are empty. Nothing is moving. The stores are closed.

———

Write a diatribe inside the story about how a prompt is a useful tool as long as it is self-created, out of your own imagination, and explain how Eudora Welty—maybe it was her, maybe not—said she could get an idea for a story from seeing a wisteria bush, or an old rocking chair, or the look on a child's face outside some gas station, and then go full tilt into the crazy wildness of your desire to nail down what it seemed like, that day a few years ago, going under the railroad tracks and then along the road to the old housing complex, weathered and beaten down, hidden off on the edge of town, to visit your sister. Mounting the old splintery stairway to her apartment, while below the drug dealers lurked and leaned on the cars, and you said to yourself, going up the stairs, before she opened the door, I have to use this as a prompt, this moment here, before she opens the door, to write a story about someone like this, placed in public housing, alone, struggling with her illness, and use that thought to end the story, leaving behind a frank admission—somehow—that everything you create is fueled by such moments and is also useless, because reality has a blunt force that is too brutal to put into words: because words are too formal, too structured. Then, in an unleashing of spirit, admit that by giving up, only by giving up, can you find the stories that might convey that moment, the one you're in, and then approach the door and begin to knock, waiting for her to open up, to present her beautiful face to you.